Merry Christmas

emie

Van Achte

Have a great
Holiday

Greater Than
ANGELS

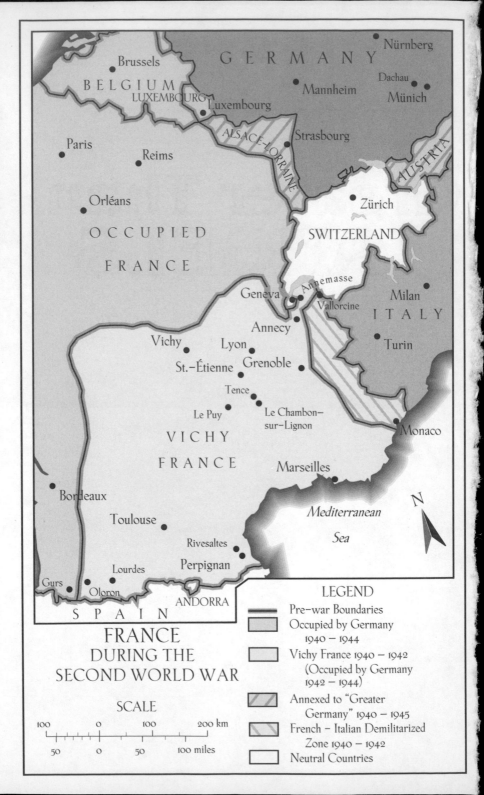

Nürnberg

GERMANY

Brussels

BELGIUM

LUXEMBOURG

Luxembourg

Dachau

Mannheim

Münich

ALSACE-LORRAINE

Strasbourg

Paris

Reims

AUSTRIA

Orléans

Zürich

SWITZERLAND

OCCUPIED

FRANCE

Annemasse

Geneva

Milan

Vallorcine

ITALY

Annecy

Vichy

Lyon

Turin

St.-Étienne

Grenoble

Tence

Le Puy

Le Chambon-
sur-Lignon

Monaco

VICHY

FRANCE

Marseilles

Bordeaux

Mediterranean

Toulouse

Sea

N

Rivesaltes

Perpignan

Lourdes

Gurs

Oloron

SPAIN

ANDORRA

LEGEND

Pre-war Boundaries

Occupied by Germany
1940 – 1944

Vichy France 1940 – 1942
(Occupied by Germany
1942 – 1944)

Annexed to "Greater
Germany" 1940 – 1945

French – Italian Demilitarized
Zone 1940 – 1942

Neutral Countries

FRANCE
DURING THE
SECOND WORLD WAR

SCALE

100   0   100   200 km

50   0   50   100 miles

Greater Than
ANGELS

CAROL MATAS

Scholastic Canada Ltd.
Toronto, New York, London, Sydney, Auckland

Scholastic Canada Ltd.
175 Hillmount Road, Markham, Ontario L6C 1Z7

Scholastic Inc.
555 Broadway, New York, NY 10012, USA

Scholastic Australia Pty Limited
PO Box 579, Gosford, NSW 2250, Australia

Scholastic New Zealand Ltd.
Private Bag 94407, Greenmount, Auckland, New Zealand

Scholastic Ltd.
Villiers House, Clarendon Avenue, Leamington Spa,
Warwickshire CV32 5PR, UK

Canadian Cataloguing in Publication Data
Matas, Carol, 1949-
Greater than angels
ISBN 0-590-12498-6
1. World War, 1939-1945 — Jewish resistance — France — Juvenile fiction.
I. Title.
PS8576.A7994G73 1998 jC813'.54 C98-931017-5
PZ7.M42396Gr 1998

5 4 3 2 1   Printed and bound in Canada   8 9 /9 0 1 2 /0

For Hanne Liebmann, Max Liebmann, Egon Gruenhut,
Jack Lewin, and Eva Lewin,
with thanks

ACKNOWLEDGMENTS

First, a huge thank-you to those who shared their stories with me. Never have I encountered such generosity of spirit: Hanne Liebmann, Max Liebmann, Egon Gruenhut, and Jack Lewin. Much of this story is their story. Nelly Trocmé Hewett, the daughter of André and Magda Trocmé, very kindly read my manuscript and gave a detailed critique, correcting many of my unwitting mistakes. Eva Fogelman, author of Conscience and Courage, helped me find the people to interview and gave of her time to discuss the altruistic personality. Pnina Zilberman, director of the Holocaust Education and Memorial Center of Toronto, led me to Eva, and read the manuscript for accuracy—as did all those I interviewed. Also thanks to the staff of the library and archives of the U.S. Holocaust Memorial Museum, where I viewed the video of Elizabeth Koenig and read about many others who had lived through those times.

Perry Nodelman read the manuscript and gave me an invaluable critique. My editor, David Gale, and his assistant, Michael Conathan, at Simon & Schuster, and Diane Kerner, at Scholastic Canada, were helpful, supportive, and a delight to work with. My husband, Per Brask, listened to the manuscript, chapter by chapter, and also helped me with translations from the German, particularly Egon Gruenhut's diary, written during the war.

Pierre Sauvage's documentary, Weapons of the Spirit, is an invaluable aid for anyone who wants to know about this time, as is Philip Hallie's book, Lest Innocent Blood Be Shed.

My friend Janeen Kobrinsky came up with the title and the quote from which it is taken during a fun weekend of brainstorming in Fargo, North Dakota.

Thanks to Donna Babcock for typing the manuscript and to Tim Babcock for all his help.

Finally, I would like to thank the Manitoba Arts Council and the Canada Council for grants which enabled me to do my research in New York and Washington, D.C.

One who saves a single life within
humanity is as if they had saved all humanity.

—Sanhedrin

ONE

We but teach bloody instructions, which, being taught,
return to plague the inventor.
—Shakespeare, *Macbeth*

THE DOGS BEGIN TO BARK and then ten-year-old Guy bursts through the kitchen door. "Germans!"

Klara's face turns white, the blood draining from her cheeks. I feel like I can't breathe.

Madame Debard doesn't hesitate. "This way," she says. She takes Klara and me to the side of the house. All I can see is a woodpile. "Help me, Guy," she orders. They pull the woodpile away from the house and I realize it has been wired together and hollowed out. She motions for us to crouch against the wall. We do. Madame Debard and Guy push the woodpile back in place. Everything is dark. My heart is pounding; I'm in a cold sweat. I can hear Klara's breath: short, panicky. We dare not speak. The dogs' barking gets louder and louder. The Germans have come looking for us.

If we're captured the farmers hiding us might be killed on the spot. And we'll be killed too. Maybe now, maybe later. I try to slow my breathing. I can't die now! I promised Mother I wouldn't. She was always making me promise things. I think it was the only way she knew to keep me out of trouble after Father died when I was eight.

"Promise me, Anni." (How many times had I told her to call me Anna, but she always used the baby version instead.) Promise me this or that, she'd say, and it was always *just* before I was about to do something I *really* wanted to do.

She said exactly that when this whole nightmare started. It was October 1940. We lived in Mannheim, Germany. I had been to the store to buy our meager ration of bread and when I returned home Mother met me at the door of our apartment. "Promise me," she'd said, "you won't say *anything* to them. Promise. No sarcastic comments. You don't have to prove your bravery to anyone."

"What are you talking about?"

"The Gestapo. They're in the apartment."

My mouth went so dry I could hardly get the words out. "I promise."

She took my hand and led me into the apartment. It was a small apartment, only three rooms, but there were six men in it. Six! Four were Gestapo, the dreaded secret state police. The other two were local police.

"We have to pack," Mother said. "Help Oma." Oma, Mother's mother, was living with us, as was Mother's sister, Mina. "Aunt Mina and I will do our clothes and the food." She paused. "We're leaving."

She must have seen the rage in my eyes. She held up a finger. "You promised," she said.

She hadn't needed my promise. My mind was blank. I tried to think of some cutting quote from the classics, some sophisticated yet razor-sharp thing to say. But I could only think that we were being sent away from the only home I knew.

"Is it just us?" I whispered to Mother. Perhaps they'd discovered Aunt Mina's secret work—the sewing she did for customers even though Jews weren't allowed to work. Maybe we were being arrested for that.

"No," Mother said, "it's *all* the Jews."

"Hurry up!" snapped one of the Gestapo.

Thank you, God, I said to myself, for helping Ilse and Max get away. Ilse is my older sister and Max my older brother. Oma had pull with Herr Friedler, who was one of the ministers of our region, Baden, and he'd gotten them visas. Ilse is in England; Max is in America. I'd even had a visa. But just before I was to go to England, war broke out and that was that. I wasn't allowed to leave. Although no one has actually told me, I think Oma's influence is so strong because Herr Friedler is actually Mother's *real* father. Of course they've all tried to hide it, but I'm rather an expert at eavesdropping late at night when they think I'm asleep. From what I can gather, Oma married Opa *after* Mother was born and then they had Mina. Oma had been on the stage and had had an affair with this important politician, Herr Friedler. Which, naturally, is why Mother won't let *me* become a performer.

"I won't let what happened to your grandmother happen to you!" Mother would say. "It's not a life for a nice girl." And so I'd have to sneak off to the theater instead of telling her the truth. She forced me into a life of intrigue.

The thing is, sneaking around when you *choose* to do it, is one thing. Hiding in a woodpile for fear of your life is quite another. I notice that it's not quite as dark in here as I thought it was at first. The cracks between the logs must be letting a tiny amount of light in, and I can breathe quite easily now so air must be circulating as well. I wonder how long we'll be here? The Nazis could look for hours, they could even stay on the farm all day waiting for us to crack and give ourselves up, or for the farmers to crack and turn us in. I have to stay calm and so does Klara. I can feel she is trembling. I put my mouth right up to her ear.

"Think about something," I whisper. "Anything. Keep your mind busy." I try to think of something to help her. "Pretend you're telling your children what happened to you in the war. Pretend it's all over and you're married and you're telling your children."

She squeezes my hand and nods. She takes a deep breath. If we could talk, we could tell each other out loud, but we can't take the risk. Maybe I should do the same thing. I'll try to remember everything. It'll keep my mind busy so I won't start to imagine what they'll do to us if they capture us.

In fact, if I can remember everything, then maybe when the war is over, I could make a play out of it. Of course, no one will believe it could have happened this way, so when the play is over I'll leap out from behind the curtain and declare, "All this really happened! Just like this!" And the audience, say, in America where I'll be living, will gasp and say, "No, no, it couldn't!" And I'll say, "Just like this!"

I have to start at the beginning.

That day the Gestapo came for us, I helped Oma with her packing before I went to do mine. She was eighty-seven years old and very frail. But not so frail that she didn't walk up to one of the Gestapo agents and demand to be allowed to speak to Minister Friedler. The guard laughed at her. Then he said, "Why would a German minister dirty himself by talking to a Jew?" He looked at her with such disgust, as if she were some kind of rat, not a person at all. At that moment I knew how bad the danger was because if you aren't a person anymore, why, they can do anything to you. Anything. And not feel bad about it. I wouldn't feel bad if I killed a rat—ugly, disgusting, germ infested. I'd feel like I'd done the right thing.

"Oma," I said, "come tell me what I should pack of yours." Gently I drew her away from him and sat her on her bed. I tried to keep her busy then, thinking about the packing, but her mind didn't seem to want to focus. She was in some kind of shock, being talked to like that by the Nazi, and couldn't seem to get out of it. Like he'd crushed her or something.

Mother came into the room. "One of the policemen," she said, "has offered to go to the hospital to see if Oma can go there instead of on the train. That gives us a little extra time to pack because they can't make us leave until he gets back. Anni, I've put some crystal on the dining room table. I'd promised Mrs. Koch across the street that she could have it if we were sent away. Can you take it over to her?"

I hurried into the other room, picked up the box from the table, and walked out. The men didn't try to stop me. It occurred to me that I could just run away, hide somewhere. But where? Anyway, Mother and Oma needed me.

I didn't even have to knock on Mrs. Koch's door. She'd

obviously been looking out through her curtains and opened the door as soon as I got there.

"Come in, come in." She saw the crystal. Tears came to her eyes. "Thank your mother. Tell her . . . I'm sorry."

I put the box on the floor.

"Anna," she said, "I spoke to my husband this morning. I can't tell you how but he's managed to find out where you're going."

"Where?" I asked. I dreaded to hear the name of one of the concentration camps.

"To the south of France."

"The south of France?" I repeated. "Is that a joke?"

"Not at all. He's quite sure his information is correct."

I brightened. "Well, that's not so bad then, is it?" I said.

"It doesn't sound too bad," she said, but she didn't seem convinced.

I said good-bye and hurried back to the apartment. The south of France. Nice. Cannes. Why, we could settle there in that balmy climate, and we could get work. Things were bound to be better there. Here, in Mannheim, we weren't allowed to do anything anymore—no movies, no theater (even though I snuck in anyway), no swimming. Mother's little button shop was taken away years ago and given to a German who wasn't Jewish. But in France I could go to the theater again! Maybe Aunt Mina could get her old job back sewing costumes for the theater. And Mother could work in any kind of shop.

I ran into the apartment and began packing. I'd be glad to leave! I had no non-Jewish friends left. They had all dropped me years ago—some because their parents thought it was too dangerous for them to keep a Jewish friend; some because they began to see all Jews as disgusting. They'd turn their backs to me when they saw me coming. All my Jewish friends would probably be on the transport.

"Take my shroud. Take my shroud." Oma pointed to the closet where she kept her burial shroud. She had bought it herself on her eightieth birthday—she was a practical woman and had wanted to choose the shroud she'd be buried in. But she never looked like she had any intention of dying.

I paused for a moment to think, and looked at her suitcase. "No, Oma," I said, "there's no room. Warm sweaters and stockings and skirts are more important."

She didn't exactly argue. She just kept repeating herself as if she hadn't heard me. Oma had gotten old, of course, but her mind had always been sharp. I didn't like to hear her muttering to herself like that, but I couldn't stop and worry about it then. I finished packing her suitcase and started on my own. I took lots of warm clothes, but also some pretty silk blouses and light skirts because it could be very mild in France. And I packed the beautiful leather briefcase Aunt Mina had bought me for my fifteenth birthday in August. It was a soft rectangular piece of brown leather, which closed at the top with a zipper. It lay flat in the suitcase and took up almost no room—and I would probably need it for work.

The policeman came back and said Oma would not be allowed to go to the hospital. *Pigs,* I thought. *Forcing an old woman out of her house, on a long journey like this.* Later, Mother told me the policeman had known all along they'd say no. He'd just gone to the hospital so we'd have more time to pack. He tried to help in his little way, I suppose.

After that we only had a few more minutes to close our suitcases. Some of the Gestapo guards yelled at us to hurry up. One of them put a bunch of documents on the dining room table and ordered Mother and Aunt Mina to sign.

"What are they?" Aunt Mina asked.

"They are papers signing your apartment and all its contents over to the government."

"I won't!" Aunt Mina exclaimed.

"Then," said the Gestapo guard, "you can go to platform six when we get to the station. Munich, then Dachau."

We all knew about Dachau. It was a concentration camp. Aunt Mina signed.

We had to carry our bags and bundles down the stairs and somehow get Oma down too. Six men, and not one of them helped us.

I had my suitcase in one hand and I put my other arm around Oma's back. Mother did the same. Aunt Mina carried Oma's suitcase. As we staggered down the stairs I decided that I would not let those Nazis think they'd intimidated us. They couldn't crush *my* spirit. So, in a loud voice, I told a joke to Mother, Aunt Mina, and Oma that I'd heard at the cabaret the week before.

"A woman visits a dressmaker one day," I said.

Mother glared at me to be quiet, but I ignored her.

"The woman," I continued, "has some exquisite material with her and asks the dressmaker to make her a dress. The dressmaker agrees. The woman returns in a week to collect the dress, but it isn't ready. She returns two weeks later, but still it isn't ready. Finally, after six weeks, the dress is finished. She tries it on. It is perfect! She looks like a queen in it!

"Still, when it comes time to pay she can't help but make a small jibe. 'You know,' she says to the dressmaker, 'God made the world in six days. And you took six weeks to make one dress!'

"'True,' says the dressmaker, 'but look at this dress, and look at the world!'"

Aunt Mina let out a nervous giggle. The policeman who had gone to the hospital for Oma laughed out loud, then looked around as if he might get in trouble. The others pretended they hadn't heard me. But I know they did. They couldn't shut *me* up!

When we got out onto the street we saw other families, carrying suitcases, walking past us in the direction of the train station. I recognized my friend Esther's family immediately, all those little children she was constantly babysitting, crying, scared, as their parents hurried along with them. We had no time to speak to anyone. The guards were yelling, "Schnell, schnell. Hurry up, hurry up." A truck was parked in front of our house and it already had people in it. A Gestapo guard gestured for us to get in. The truck was open in the back, but there were no stairs up into it and Oma couldn't exactly scramble up, and we weren't strong enough to lift her. None of the men would help us.

Neighbors came out of their houses to watch. And they laughed. They thought it was funny that we couldn't get her on the truck. Funny. Finally the same policeman who laughed at my joke gave her a kind of shove and she was aboard. They drove us away from our home then, under the

yellow leaves of October, the sun shining down as if nothing in the world were wrong, and I smiled at my mother and
my aunt and my grandmother and told them that everything
would be better in the south of France. Even though,
inside, a part of me couldn't believe that they would actually send us away, even after all they'd done to the Jews.

"Pack my shroud," Oma kept repeating. "Pack my
shroud."

Two

I could a tale unfold whose lightest words
Would harrow up thy soul, freeze thy young blood,
Make thy two eyes, like stars, start from their
spheres.
—Shakespeare, *Hamlet*

I SAT ON THE TRAIN and tried to think of a good joke. Something to lighten the mood as we pulled out of the station in an old French passenger car, with hard wooden benches and grimy windows.

Karl, one of the stars of the cabaret, had told a whole series of doctor jokes the other night on stage, and I'd memorized them all.

I began: " 'Doctor,' Heinrich whimpered, 'I think I'm losing my mind!' "

Mother shook her head, but Aunt Mina encouraged me. "Go ahead, Anni," she said.

I went on. " 'Look on the bright side,' the doctor replied, 'at least you won't miss it.' "

Aunt Mina smiled.

"Have you heard about cross-eyed Gertrude, who went to the eye doctor?"

Aunt Mina shook her head.

"Well, it seems she tried to kill her husband with a look but killed another man instead!"

Aunt Mina grinned. Mother smiled just a little. Maybe it was working.

" 'What's the best way to avoid diseases caused by biting dogs?' Fagey asked the doctor.

"The doctor replied, 'Don't bite any.' "

Aunt Mina giggled. Mother groaned. "Really, Anni, that's so old!"

I smiled. At least I'd gotten Mother to speak—if only to be cross at me. But Oma didn't seem to hear a word I said.

She kept muttering to herself. I couldn't hear what she was saying, but I'd never seen her behave that way—like she was suddenly *old*. She didn't even seem to realize where we were or what was happening. I suppose I should've stayed with her and tried to calm her down but seeing her like that got me so upset that I bolted from my seat. I decided to walk through the car to see if any of my friends were on it. A Gestapo soldier stood at the front of the car, quite near us. I walked toward the back. I saw a number of families whom we knew fairly well and I said hello to them. Finally, I spotted my friend Klara and her older brother, Rudi, with their mother and father. Klara and I had been best friends until I began spending time at the cabaret. Klara is from a very wealthy, refined family and she's been overprotected all her life. She is timid and would never disobey her parents, so she refused to go with me to the shows.

When I was supposed to be at her house, I really would be at the cabaret on Holzwegstrasse. I always used her for my alibi because Mother didn't know I wasn't seeing her much anymore. The cabaret had singers, dancers, comics. It wasn't *serious* theater—they didn't perform my favorite writer, Bertolt Brecht, or my other favorite, Shakespeare—they did fun stuff, cutting and political. I look older than my age, being very tall at five feet nine inches, and I have rather good legs. Because of that, sometimes they let me put on a costume and sing in the chorus line if one of the girls called in sick. So I was almost like an understudy. And I *can* sing. We had a very good choir in school so I got coaching from an early age. My dancing isn't quite as good because Mother would never let me take lessons. I have comedic timing too.

"How are you?" I asked Klara, swaying and catching onto the seat. I was really glad to see her, more than I cared to admit, I think, even to myself. Suddenly I didn't feel quite so alone.

I could see Klara had been crying. Her mother still was.

"How should we be?" Mrs. Engel said.

"And your family? They are in good health?" Mr. Engel asked. He was always a gentleman. He had owned a huge department store downtown until it was stolen from him by the Nazis. And he'd been a leader in the Jewish community of Mannheim ever since I could remember.

"Yes, thank you, Mr. Engel."

"Hullo, legs," murmured Rudi.

Rudi was two years older than me, and I considered him a pest. Just the opposite of Klara, he was always in trouble for one thing or another.

"Hullo, clown," I muttered back. He had bright red hair and freckles and was around six feet three but skinny—he looked something like a clown. "Where's your red nose?"

"What was that, dear?" Mrs. Engel asked.

"Oh, nothing. I just told Rudi that I hoped I hadn't tread on his toes," I said, and then purposefully lurched toward him and stepped right on his foot.

"Ow!"

"Oops. So clumsy. So sorry." I smiled sweetly at Rudi.

"Oh, how *can* you two," Klara said, and she began to cry again.

"Listen, Klara, I have a joke for you." What else do you do to stop someone crying? Make them laugh. I plunged in before anyone could stop me. "A young girl goes to the zoo on her first-ever visit. And there she sees something right out of the Bible. 'And the calf and the lion shall lie down together, and none shall be afraid.' You see, there is a calf in the lion's cage. She can't believe it. She spots a zoo worker and asks, 'Have the lion and the calf been in that cage together very long?'

" 'Yes,' is the reply, 'over a year!'

" 'That's amazing.'

" 'Of course, every morning we put in a new calf!' "

I waited for a laugh but didn't get one. Instead Mr. Engel sighed. "Rather like us to the Nazis, that calf," he said. Klara cried harder.

"Good for you," Rudi said. "You really cheered her up."

I managed to give him a little kick in the shin before I left. "We're just up there, Klara," I said. "Come visit me if you can." Klara nodded through her tears. I said good-bye to her parents and went back to my family.

As I neared our seats I could hear Oma demanding in a loud voice, "Put me to bed. Get me undressed. Take off my shoes. I want to go to bed." Mother was trying to reason with her.

"Mother, dear, we're on a train now. It's going to be a long trip. But as soon as we get off, you'll go to bed." Oma didn't seem to even hear her. She continued to go on and on.

The Gestapo guard shouted at my mother. "Shut her up! She's getting on my nerves."

"What can I do?" said my mother. "She's lost her mind from all this."

"Do something," he barked, "or I'll throw her off the train myself. She's giving me a headache."

Mother gripped my arm. "He means it, Anni. He'd do it. You must find a doctor. She needs a sedative. Quickly!"

I turned around again and moved through the car, asking everyone if there was a doctor on the train. When I reached the Engel family I told them what had happened. Rudi actually managed to be helpful.

"There's a doctor two cars down," he said. When he saw my inquiring look he answered, "I made sure to find out if there was one aboard in case Mother or Father needed help."

I guess my eyebrows must have gone up even further.

"Is that out of character?" he asked. He knows I'm crazy about theater.

"The wonderful thing about well-drawn characters," I retorted, "is that they are always full of surprises."

"Touché," he said. I hurried through the cars until I found the doctor. He was a fairly young man, with thick black hair and small round glasses perched on a long, slightly crooked nose. He looked exhausted and was bending over a young child who was crying.

"Excuse me," I said.

He looked up. "Not now," he snapped. "I'm busy. Can't you see?"

Well, yes, I *could* see, but Oma needed him and I wasn't going anywhere.

"I'll wait," I said.

The doctor spoke to the little boy's mother. "It's just a cold. Try to keep him warm and give him as much to drink as you can."

"But we only have a thermos of tea," the mother wailed. "When that's gone, then what?"

The doctor shook his head. "I don't know," he said. "You still here?" he asked as he straightened up.

"It's my grandmother," I explained. "She's . . . I don't know. It's as if she's suddenly lost her mind. Is that possible?"

"What is her age?"

"Eighty-seven."

"It's possible at any age, but the old ones are having a very hard time accepting all this as reality. It's so much like a nightmare that their brains seem to have concluded that it is. That it's not real." He grabbed his bag. "Let's have a look."

When we got back the Gestapo guard was obviously far more agitated.

"Shut her up!" he shrieked.

Oma's voice was even louder and had a terrible whine to it. "I want to go to bed. Now. Get me undressed!" And then she'd start to undress and Mother and Aunt Mina would have to grab her hands.

The doctor felt her forehead, looked in her eyes, listened to her chest. Then he kneeled down by my mother and spoke very quietly. I kneeled down too so I could hear him.

"If we can't keep her quiet, they might shoot her. Or worse. They might really throw her off the train." Mother went pale. "Here's a vial of sleeping pills. Two will quiet her for a couple of hours. The entire amount will quiet her for much longer."

My mother grasped Aunt Mina's hand. He couldn't mean that there were enough there to kill her, could he? But yes, I could see from Mother's face that was exactly what he meant. I wanted to throw myself at the Nazi and kill him with my bare hands. Why didn't we? There was only one of him. But of course he had the machine gun. He could kill us all before one of us got to him.

"Thank you, doctor," Mother whispered.

"I'm sorry," he said.

Mother nodded.

We had two water flasks, and Mother put the pills in her hands and looked at Aunt Mina. Aunt Mina nodded.

"No!" I whispered.

"We have no choice," Mother whispered back. "If I give her only two she'll wake up and start all over again. Do you want to see her thrown off the train? Left to die in agony in some ditch? You heard how they beat Professor Cohen to death last week—in the street, in front of everybody! You think the guard wouldn't do it?"

Tears welled up in my eyes. How could things have come to this?

Before Mother could change her mind she fed all the pills to Oma.

Within minutes Oma was fast asleep. I sat with her then. And held her hand. And listened to her breathing. Oma had been my best and closest friend from the time I could remember anything. She'd always encouraged my love of theater and singing and the arts. She knew where I really was at night, I never kept anything from *her*. And she'd discuss Shakespeare with me, and Molière, and Chekhov, and Ibsen, and we would analyze the plays and the parts. When I landed my first leading role in school she coached me. That was the last part I did before I was thrown out of the public school for being a Jew. And we used to laugh—I'd tell her the jokes from the cabaret. *Nothing* ever shocked her. She had a roar of a laugh. She'd bellow and slap her leg when she found something funny. She had worked in the theater herself until she was seventy-five years old—and she made a good living from it, too.

I gazed at the frail little woman slumped against the seat. I looked at my mother, her face set in pain, and at Aunt Mina, who had tears silently gliding down her cheeks. And at the Nazi guard.

Where does evil come from, I wondered. How had that man gotten to the point where he could even *consider* throwing her off the train? Had the entire world been taken over by evil? It felt that way. And how could killing someone be an act of mercy? Or was it?

I must have dozed. Day became night. Suddenly, I woke. At first I thought I was dreaming. Then I realized it was Oma talking. "Get me undressed. Get me to bed." She hadn't died! The pills hadn't worked! I threw my arms around her and kissed her. Mother looked frantically around for the Gestapo guard. But by some miracle, he had changed position and was now standing guard at the other end of the train car.

"You can go to bed soon, Oma," I said. "Soon." I knew that hundreds of thousands of Jews had fled to France already to escape the Nazis. And when no other country would take them in, the French had. Even the United States had turned away most Jews. But not France. France was a great and generous country. So I dreamed of a country bathed in sunlight, and how the French people would save us. But nothing is so simple, is it?

THREE

Man, I can assure you, is a nasty creature.
—Molière, *Le Tartuffe*

FOR TWO DAYS WE HAD no food, just what we'd brought and that was soon gone, and no water, once our flasks were empty. On the second day we stopped at a station. We begged the guard to let us get off for water. He refused. Another old person in the car lost his mind on the second day. I stayed with Oma and tried to keep her calm. The only blessing was that the Gestapo guard left us alone. I wondered if it was possible that he had been so mean because he actually felt bad when he saw the state Oma was in. I'll never know. I suppose one or two of the guards might not have liked their jobs. Most did though. You could see it. They were heartless.

It was late in the afternoon of the second day when we stopped at a small station in the French countryside. Oma was getting worse, crying, babbling, and I was in a panic, terrified that the Gestapo guard was going to hurt her. I kept a wary eye on him. Suddenly, he stalked down the train from the other end, heading straight for us. I stood up. He'd have to fight me to get to her! Mother pulled on my hand, but I wouldn't budge.

The guard got closer and closer—and then pushed right past me and walked off the train! I moved over to the window and tried to see through the grimy glass. All the German guards were gathering on the platform. Then another train came into the station and blocked my view. After about fifteen minutes, it left, and the platform was empty. No Gestapo!

I turned to the rest of the car and yelled, "They've gone! They've gone!" I hugged Oma. "They've gone, Oma," I said. But she didn't understand.

"I want to go to bed," she cried.

"Soon," I said. "Soon."

Within minutes the entire car was in chaos. Everyone was arguing about what it could mean. Were we free? If so, where could we go? None of us had any money—the Gestapo had taken all our German money and exchanged it for only two thousand French francs per person. They told us that whoever carried more than that would be shot. And we didn't know anyone in France. We didn't even know exactly where we were. Should we run?

Finally Mr. Engel took charge. Everyone looked up to him and respected him, so when he walked to the front of the car and put up his hands for quiet, the yelling soon dwindled into a hushed silence.

"I am going to get off the train," he said, "and try to speak to someone in authority here."

And that's what he did. He walked off the train. I saw him talking to a train porter, then another man in uniform turned up. There were a lot of wild gestures, and a French gendarme appeared. Then more people from the other train cars—leaders from the Jewish community—gathered, until the platform was quite full of people, talking, trying to figure out what was happening. Finally Mr. Engel came back to our car.

"It appears," he said, "that the Nazis have gone back to Germany and we are left here, as refugees. But the French see us only as Germans and the French are at war with Germany so we are, apparently, *enemies*. Enemy aliens."

"But, it can't be!" someone said. "Did you tell them that we're Jews?"

"Of course I did," Mr. Engel said, obviously frustrated. "But it's not getting through. They are checking with the local prefect of the area but I suspect we will be sent to some kind of camp."

That started everyone off again. Mr. Engel went back outside to continue to try to make the authorities listen to our story.

Suddenly a young woman from our car ran to the front and leaped off the train.

"Throw me my suitcase," she called.

Quickly, Rudi, of all people, lifted her case and threw it down the steps. She grabbed it and ran across the tracks into a meadow, away from the town.

"Why don't you go, too?" I asked Rudi as he walked past me.

He glanced at my family. "Same reason you don't," he said.

He was right. They needed us to look after them.

After a long delay, Mr. Engel got back on the car shrugging, still unable to tell us what was going to happen to us. Then the train started again. Now what? It was horrible not knowing where you were going, feeling so helpless. I hated it. I couldn't just sit there. I leaped up to my feet and before I really knew what I was doing, I began to sing a song that I'd heard often in the cabaret, "Oh, How I Wish That We Were Kids Again." Soon I had everyone but Mother singing with me—but for once she didn't get mad at me for showing off.

Finally I got tired and so did everyone else. As night fell, quiet descended on our car, and that's how I remember pulling in to the station. The quiet. And the *cold*. I'd expected it to be hot, but when the doors opened, we were assaulted by freezing blasts of air. The sky was gray, cloudy, miserable. It was like the foreshadowing in a play, warning of worse things to come. We sat on the track for hours, watching out the window as trucks came and went taking people away from the other cars. Finally it was our turn. I didn't know how we were going to get Oma off the train until Rudi popped up, lifted her as if she weighed nothing, and carried her into the open truck. It was pouring rain by then and within minutes we were soaked to the bone and frozen through.

The truck screeched away from the train and proceeded to career through the streets of the town. There were no benches or seats and not enough room to sit, so we were flung about like little rag dolls. I tried to hang on to Oma and keep her from falling. I wrapped my arms around her from the back and Mother held on to me, and somehow we managed to keep her from getting hurt. We left the town and drove through the country until our driver screeched to a halt, just outside some large gates.

By then it was too dark to really see where we were. It

looked as if there were lots of large buildings, like an army base or something, maybe barracks, but I couldn't be sure. Only women had been put on our truck. They drove us through the gates, then dropped us off without our luggage. The hulking forms of buildings rose in front of us, but between the rain and the dark it was hard to make anything out. A man shouted at us to follow him. As soon as we took our first steps we sank ankle deep in mud. It was horrible. We slogged through it, almost carrying Oma, until finally we were let into a barracks. It was a long, low building with one small light at each end. There were no beds, no bunks, nothing. There was one door at each end; no windows, only wooden hatches.

We looked around in stunned disbelief. Were we *prisoners*? Where had the men been taken? The boys? What were the French going to do with us? Didn't they realize that we were no threat to them, that we hated the Nazis even more than they did? It was so ironic. To the Germans we weren't Germans, we were only Jews. They had taken away our citizenship years ago. And to the French we were Germans. The enemy.

A French guard yelled in broken German, "There's straw, barracks twenty-one, for floors. Follow me."

No one moved. The adults seemed paralyzed. I grabbed Klara and dragged her out the door.

"No!" she protested.

"Do you want your mother to sleep on the floor?" I demanded.

Some of the other young people heard me and they sort of woke up. They joined me and we followed the guard.

Again we sank into mud over our ankles. I had short boots on and mud had already oozed right into them. The girls groaned, not wanting to wade through it again. It was disgusting, but this was no time to be squeamish.

"Come on, girls," I said. "Pretend we're in a horror film and we all have the lead part of the spunky heroine. We have to slog through the dank and the dark, but behind every building some demented Nazi lurks, except coming to our rescue is a very tall, *very* handsome young man with green eyes. . . ." I continued like that all the way there. Klara actually giggled. I think it was nerves. But at one point she grabbed my hand and we walked together.

We got to a barracks where we were given straw, but not enough for everyone to sleep on. So we slogged back to our barracks, then we turned around and did it all over again. After four trips I had enough straw for Oma, Aunt Mina, and Mother. I was too tired to go back for any for me. I pulled off my boots and my stockings, which were soaked through with water and mud. I lay down on my coat. The others put their coats over the straw. We used our handbags for pillows, and somehow we finally fell asleep.

I woke up in the morning to a female guard yelling at us in French to come to the field kitchen for some breakfast. Klara quickly became our official translator as her French was excellent—mine was terrible.

I looked around. The place was packed. Women moaned and sighed as they woke up. I found out later that there were sixty women to each barracks. And there were *hundreds* of barracks. The place was huge.

Before we could eat we had to go to the bathroom. That

was easy to find. We followed the line of women and the smell. When we reached the "facility" it made me gag. It was revolting—a huge long plank with holes in the wood and movable containers on tracks underneath. It was raised six feet in the air, so the only way to get to it was up a thin ladder. Oma was too weak and too sick to climb. She'd never manage it. The first thing we had to do was get her into a hospital where, at the very least, she could use bed-pans and not have to struggle up those impossible steps.

Mother, Aunt Mina, and I went to the field kitchen. We were each given a small piece of bread and some tea.

"There is barbed wire all around the camp," I said to Mother. "This *is* a prison!"

"I know, dear," she said. "But at least it isn't a German prison. The French will take care of us."

I snorted. "If this is being taken care of, I'd hate to see what they do to people they don't like."

"But they just don't realize that we're all Jews," Mother said. "When they do, it'll be different, I'm sure."

"This is really a refugee camp, Anni," Aunt Mina said, "not a prison exactly. It's called Gurs. I've talked to a few people and found out that originally it was for Spanish refugees, many of whom are still here. And we're refugees too. The French will come to their senses. It will probably take them a few days to get organized, that's all. They'll have to find food for thousands of people and that won't be easy with the shortages everywhere."

As usual, Mother and Aunt Mina made sense. But I had learned something from the night after night I had spent with the artists at the cabaret on Holzwegstrasse: Intuition often serves you better than logic. And as I looked around, at the guards, at the barbed wire, at the horrible conditions, all my hopes of France being a better place to live than Germany tumbled down around me. And I knew that I would have to work very hard if we were all to survive. It had just been the four of us for so long now—I had to make sure nothing happened to Mother or Aunt Mina or Oma.

When I got back to our barracks I found Klara and her mother dissolved in tears on the floor. They hadn't eaten or used the latrine. Needless to say they were miserable and very uncomfortable.

"I *can't* go in there," Klara said. "I can't!"

Her mother echoed her daughter. "It's so primitive. It's beyond belief. Why, there's no paper. What are we to do?"

"You can't hold it forever," I said. "You may as well get it over with." I paused. "Wait." I ran to my mother and asked her if she had a handkerchief in her bag. She had one. And I had one. I pulled Klara and her mother up and offered them the handkerchiefs.

Mrs. Engel took a deep breath. "You're right, Anna," she said, "we have to get used to it. There's no reason for you to part with those handkerchiefs. They may as well be gold here. Klara and I will be fine."

I led them to the latrines and then to the soup kitchen, where they were given tea in old tin cans. Mrs. Engel started to cry again. As we slogged through the mud, her beautiful suede boots were ruined within minutes. She didn't care though, she was too worried about Rudi and Mr. Engel.

"Klara and I will try to find out where they are," I offered.

"Oh, Anna, would you?"

"Of course we will, won't we, Klara?"

Klara looked at me and I could tell she didn't have the will to fight me. She was as small as I was tall, taking after her mother, just like Rudi took after his father. Her hair was red, like Rudi's, but with a lot of brown shades, and she had deep green eyes, just like he did. But whereas he usually looked silly, she was very beautiful. Heads had always turned when we were together, because with my height and long black hair and big brown eyes, I suppose we made a sort of striking pair.

"Come on," I said.

It had stopped raining, thankfully, so we just had the mud to deal with. We trudged around the barracks until we came to the barbed wire, which separated us from the other blocks. We could see men and boys on the other side. I yelled as loud as I could.

"Are you from Baden?"

A young boy called back, "Yes!"

"Are you all there, from the trains?"

"I think so, yes. And are the women all there too?"

"We are! Everyone is here. But no luggage."

"No luggage here, either!"

Well, that was the basics taken care of. We were able to report back to Mrs. Engel that all the men were somewhere in the camp. She seemed relieved.

The first thing everyone wanted was to let our families know where we were. We had cousins in Berlin, Father's brothers and their families. We had my sister in England, my brother in America. The guards told us that we could write letters and send telegrams, so we waited anxiously for our bags because we'd all packed writing papers and pens. When the luggage finally appeared it was dumped in one spot, outside, in the mud. My suitcase had been opened and my beautiful lace blouses were gone. But my leather briefcase was still there, and so were my stockings and my skirts. Mother's suitcase never showed up. Aunt Mina's was almost intact. Oma's was crushed and so waterlogged we weren't sure we could salvage anything. It was chaos as everyone tried to find their own things. Some fought over bags, and many more wept. The little they had left was now in ruins.

For a moment I stood, holding on to my briefcase. What a fool I'd been to pack it. I'd never use it to go to a new job, or to school; that was obvious. Much as I loved it, now it was a nasty reminder of our ruined hopes. For one moment I had an overwhelming urge to drop it in the mud with the rest of the mess of our former lives. Instead, a defiant voice inside me said, "Keep it. And as long as you have it, you'll have hope." So I kept it.

Luckily, Aunt Mina's writing paper had remained dry. Mother managed to get three letters written, and the French matron who supervised our barracks collected hers with the others later that day.

As everyone in the barracks wrote their letters I told them one of my very favorite jokes.

"Question: 'What's a Jewish telegram?'

"Answer: 'Letter to follow. Start worrying.'"

I got a lot of laughs from that one.

It took a few days, but the authorities finally managed to get us more straw and cotton to cover it so no one had to sleep directly on the floor. Since I'd been on the ground for three nights, I was pretty happy with my new "mattress."

Also on the third day we went for our first wash. Water ran in open troughs, like ones horses drink from, near a barracks right off the main road. I had to take off my shirt right there in the open to wash. I had no choice. Klara and Mrs. Engel were with us, but Klara refused. Mother talked to them.

"Klara, dear, would you rather wash or have lice?"

"Lice?"

"Of course. Look around. We have to make every effort to stay clean."

"I saw two rats this morning," I declared.

"Oooh!" Klara groaned.

"You see," Mother said, gently prodding Mrs. Engel. "We don't have time to be proud."

Klara gave in, but Mrs. Engel just couldn't. Not that day, anyway.

We managed to get Oma in a special medical barracks. It wasn't a hospital, but there were other old people there and the block started to get volunteers to look after them.

So after the first few days, a little bit of order grew out of the chaos. Oma was settled, and even had a bed in the building she was in, and a routine began to develop. Still, for some reason a line from a song in *The Threepenny Opera* kept going through my head: "Oh, the shark has pretty teeth, dear, and he shows them pearly white." The sharks were everywhere. Were we their dinner?

FOUR

Oh, the shark has pretty teeth, dear,
And he shows them pearly white.
—Bertolt Brecht, *The Threepenny Opera*

IT IS SO CRAMPED, curled up against the wall, hidden by the woodpile. I would give anything to be able to stretch my legs.

Klara whispers in my ear. "I feel like we've been in here for hours. How much longer, do you think?"

I whisper back. "I don't know. I don't hear *anything* anymore, and it must be three or four o'clock by now. Still, I know Madame Debard will let us out as soon as it's safe, so it must not be safe."

"What are you thinking about?" Klara asks.

"Gurs. What about you?"

"Me too. I was thinking about your concerts."

"I hear something!" I hiss. "Quiet!"

Twigs snap, I can hear the crunch of boots on the ground. As long as they don't torture me, I think. Just let them shoot me. I don't think I could stand up to torture for more than a minute. Then I'd tell them anything. Anything.

I'm having trouble breathing again. I have an overwhelming urge to burst out of this tiny space, even if it's into the arms of the Gestapo. Why not get it over with?

The concerts. I'll think about the concerts.

❖ ❖ ❖

Every block had an administration barracks and Mother worked in ours because of her experience running her own business. The French had to keep track of who lived, who died, rations. Also, people were allowed to have money sent to them from relatives outside the camp, but a black market in food and medicine grew that was terribly unfair to those who had no money coming in. So Mr. Engel helped set up a kind of banking method. People were allowed to spend a fixed amount of money every month, but they also paid a small tax so the ones who had nothing could be looked after. Mother worked in the office with three other women, helping to administer all of this.

By December, people started to die of starvation. Often I'd go to help Mother and every day the men, Jews from another block, would kick at the door and ask: "You got something for us?" They meant bodies. I never got used to that. They seemed so callous.

After a while the French guards were replaced by local civilians who lived in barracks outside the camp. I happen to know that although they carried guns there were no bullets in them. I knew because I used to chat with one of them—to try to learn French. And he confided in me. Of course I told everyone, but still, even though there were no bullets, where could we run?

But my mind is wandering. The concerts. How did they start? It was Oma, of course. I went to visit her every day. Getting a pass was easy: Mother could just give me one. However, I didn't mention it to anyone in the barracks except Klara so that people wouldn't resent my having extra privileges. Oma slowly came back to herself after a couple weeks and seemed to know where she was and recognize me and everything.

"This is a terrible place, Anni," she'd say to me. That's how she started off our conversation every day.

"I know, Oma." She was right, it was terrible. It was still filthy. We had to hang our clothes on lines strung up on nails to save them from the rats. We were given electric light two hours every night, from six to eight, otherwise we lived in darkness. There was one stove, which was lit for two hours each day, and the women would fight over whose turn it was to use it to heat a cup of water for tea. I never would have thought that a cup of tea would be something to fight over. We were fed almost nothing—some watery soup at lunch, some watery soup at dinner. If there were vegetables in the soup they were ones I'd *never* have eaten at home—like turnips. Sometimes they fed us horse meat. Or cow udders. I never could have imagined how horrible it was to be hungry. Not hungry the way you are just before dinner. Hungry so it hurts. And no end to it in sight. It was much later that we discovered that the camp director and a few others had been taking money from the government meant for our food and keeping it for themselves. As far as I'm concerned, that makes them murderers.

"I'm going to die here," Oma would continue. "I wish you'd brought my shroud."

"Oma, you aren't going to die here. They'll let us out soon."

Except I was lying. By then I knew that as long as the war was on they wouldn't let us out. Mother had found out quite a bit since she'd been working in the office. A law passed by the Vichy government on October 4 gave prefects, or heads of departments, the right to intern foreign Jews and keep them there. It was odd the way France was being run since the Germans invaded in June. The northern half of the country was occupied by Germans, but the southern part wasn't. Marshal Pétain ran the Vichy government in the south, called the Free Zone. That's where Gurs was situated. But Pétain had a policy of collaborating with the Germans. He seemed to have decided that to get in the Nazis' good books he'd go after the Jews. Most of the foreign-born Jews living in France already had their citizenship taken away, even though, before the war, the French had promised *never* to do that. In fact, quite a lot of these Jews were in the camp with us. They were being arrested all over France. And they had thought France was their home, that France would protect them. Not if they were Jews! Of course, not all the French liked Pétain. General de Gaulle had escaped to England and was trying to create a resistance movement, the Free French Forces. I wished I could escape and join him. I wanted to fight!

Oma would pat her bed with a nervous motion, over and over. "No, dear. I'm going to die here. Why didn't you bring my shroud?"

I had to get her off the topic.

"Guess what?" I'd said. "Sonia Morenthal is in my barracks!"

"The violinist from the Munich symphony?"

"Yes," I nodded. "She was living not far from here and was caught in a roundup."

"Well, well," Oma said. "You should make a concert."

"But she has no instrument," I said.

"Well, dear," Oma said, "find her one."

What else did I have to do with my time?

That night there was a service planned in the field because it was erev Hanukkah and everyone in the camp was allowed to go. I would be able to talk to some of the leaders that would be there.

It was a cold night as we all crowded onto the field. The men had made a huge menorah out of tin cups. Rabbi Adler lit the menorah. He was one of the rabbis who had been on the train from Baden with us. Everyone sang the blessing together, our voices rising from that field into the cold, still air, so high that maybe the sound reached the stars.

Hearing those melodies made me think of my father. And of my older brother, Max, and my older sister, Ilse. We used to go to synagogue when my father was alive. And even though men and women couldn't sit together, I remember walking there with Father, my small hand in his larger one. I remember how safe I felt. After he died Mother stopped going to synagogue. She stopped keeping a kosher household. She said she didn't believe in God anymore. But I did. Because if there was no God, then that would mean there was no Father, either. No spirit to talk to at night when you couldn't fall asleep and you didn't feel safe anymore. So I chose to keep believing. So did Max and Ilse. The three of us would go to shul almost every week. Suddenly I missed them all horribly—despite the fact that Max used to tease me mercilessly and Ilse constantly criticized me for not being enough of a lady. But

Father was gone forever, so it was him I missed most of all.

I asked Father to help us, and to watch over us because we needed his help now, badly.

After the service I managed to corner Rabbi Adler and I asked him if he knew of a way to get some instruments. He told me to speak to the volunteers from the CIMADE who had established themselves in the camp—in fact they were living in a barracks just like the rest of us. They were a Protestant group formed to help displaced persons.

The woman he pointed out to me didn't look much like a Christian volunteer—or not like I would have pictured one, anyway. She was tall, very thin, elegant, with her blond hair coiffed in a French braid. She wore a long fur coat and tiny boots with heels.

"Excuse me?" I said in French, but hearing my accent she answered me immediately in flawless German.

"Yes, dear," she said, friendly, not at all snooty.

"Rabbi Adler said I should ask you . . . well, you see, I know you're trying to get us food and clothes, well, of course, that's important, but other things are important too!"

I bit my lip. She'd probably laugh at me. She'd probably think I was really stupid.

"What other things, for instance?"

I straightened my shoulders and remembered one of Oma's favorite lines from Heinrich Heine: "A daring beginning is halfway to winning." I took a deep breath.

"Music."

She didn't laugh. Instead, she considered me thoughtfully.

"Music *is* as important as food," she agreed.

"Do you think so?" I could hardly believe my ears.

"Well, maybe not *quite* as important." She smiled.

"But it is, isn't it?" I said, my words tumbling over each other. "Because if we feel hopeless and if everything is ugly then we just *want* to die, don't we? But if we can make something beautiful, if we can make people laugh or let them remember that there is beauty still, right here, in this dung heap, then maybe that *is* as important . . ." I stopped.

She regarded me seriously. "You're quite right. What's your name?"

"Anna Hirsch."

"And mine is Françoise Lorrain."

We shook hands.

"What do you suggest, Anna?"

"Well," I said, "Sonia Morenthal is in my barracks."

"The violinist?"

"Yes!" She knew who Sonia was. She was an angel!

"Then we must find her a violin. And you, Anna, you must be an artist of some sort, to speak so passionately on the subject."

Suddenly I felt shy. I was nothing compared to the people who must be here.

"Come on," she said, "what do you do?"

"I sing a little. Tell a few jokes. Dance."

"Then we will have a concert. We will find instruments, and people to play them, and *you*, Anna, will sing."

"No! I couldn't."

She shook her head. "That has to be part of the deal. You must be part of this undertaking."

So I repeated another one of Oma's favorite sayings to myself. "Nothing ventured, nothing gained." And I said yes.

I found Klara waiting for me a little ways away and as we walked back to the barracks I told her about the conversation I'd just had. She was really proud of me. But as I talked to her I got more and more nervous. Panic-stricken, actually.

How could I, Anna Hirsch, sing with the first violinist of the Munich symphony? It was impossible. What could I have been thinking? And anyway, I didn't know any classical pieces. All I knew were cabaret songs and all of Bert Brecht's and Kurt Weill's songs, by heart.

When I got back to the barracks I marched straight over to Sonia Morenthal.

"Miss Morenthal?" I said, suddenly meek as a lamb.

"Yes?"

"Miss Morenthal, I have wonderful news. The CIMADE will find you a violin and they are going to organize a concert."

Her eyes lit up as if she'd been offered an entire meal: chicken soup, meat, and even dessert.

Now Klara is a girl who *never, ever* says anything. But she chose this moment to become a blabbermouth.

"And," Klara butted in, "Anna is going to sing with you."

"Wonderful!" exclaimed Sonia Morenthal.

"No," I said, glaring at Klara. "No. I couldn't."

"Yes, but you must. What is your repertoire?"

"That's the thing," I said, turning bright red. "I don't have one."

"You know all of *The Threepenny Opera* by heart," Klara piped in again. "She really can sing that!"

I used to force Klara to listen to me when I practiced. I'd forgotten what a good friend she'd been to me until I became too busy for her.

"But I love Kurt Weill," Miss Morenthal said. "And he's been banned by the Nazis. So, naturally, we *must* sing him. Yes, that will be our first concert. As soon as I get my violin we will practice."

The next afternoon I went to the CIMADE headquarters, a barracks in our block, and met Madame Lorrain and her coworker Madame Henri. While Madame Lorrain was tall and elegant, Madame Henri was round as a dumpling. Later, I learned that they both had families in Lyon, yet they stayed in Gurs to help us. They ushered me into the main room and I'll never forget it—there was almost an entire orchestra assembled! All tuning their instruments. And then Madame Lorrain introduced me to the original director of Brecht's *The Threepenny Opera*. I was so awestruck that I couldn't speak. Never mind sing. I wanted to *kill* Klara.

But he was so kind and he coaxed me, and said, "We really do need some singers." Two grown women appeared who were real cabaret stars, and I began to back out thinking they wouldn't need me. But they asked me to stay. So I sang a little for them, and they clapped! And then the three of us became a little choir.

It was wonderful. All that week I didn't notice that I was so hungry it hurt, or so cold or so wet that it was almost unbearable. I didn't see the filth, the rats, the misery,

I just felt the music. The pure joy of working with such great artists overwhelmed me. I don't think I'd ever been so happy!

The afternoon of the concert we played in a barracks that was partly cleared for us. Mother was there and Aunt Mina and Mr. and Mrs. Engel and Rudi and Klara, as they'd all managed to get passes, thanks to Mother's influence. I was so nervous I couldn't have eaten even if there'd been food! (In fact, I used that line all day and got quite a few laughs.) We sang "What Keeps a Man Alive" from *The Threepenny Opera*,

> *Now those among you full of pious teaching,*
> *Who teach us to renounce the major sins,*
> *Should know before you do your "heavy preaching"*
> *Our middle's empty. There it all begins—*
> *First feed the face; and then talk right and wrong*
> *For even honest folk may act like sinners,*
> *Unless they've had their customary dinners.*
> *What keeps a man alive?*
> *What keeps a man alive? He lives on others;*
> *He likes to taste them first, then eat them*
> *whole if he can.*
> *Forget that they're supposed to be his brothers,*
> *That he himself was ever called a man.*

Occasionally Madame Henri had to give a little piece of sugar to one of the musicians or a small piece of bread to a member of the audience because they would get so faint from hunger, but otherwise it was a huge success. When it was all over, everyone applauded and cheered. I really did feel weak, then. Weak but exhilarated.

"Shsh, shsh," Klara hisses.

"Sorry," I whisper. "Was I singing out loud?"

"You were humming 'What Keeps a Man Alive?'" Klara confirms.

"I was thinking about that first concert," I reply.

"I'll never forget you singing that," Klara whispers. "You were inspired." She pauses. "I can't hear the boots anymore, can you?"

"No."

"Why doesn't Madame Debard let us out?"

"The Germans must still be here, looking for us."

"We have to be quiet," Klara instructs me, for once being the sensible one. "Maybe one of them is standing out there listening. Do what you told me. Think about what's happened."

She's right. But I don't want to think about what happened next.

FIVE

O! Woe is me,
To have seen what I have seen,
see what I see!
—Shakespeare, *Hamlet*

I RAN ALL THE WAY TO Oma's barracks afterward to tell her about my triumph. It had all been her idea, after all. I showed my pass and hurried in.

One of the volunteers came up to me and barred my way. "I'm sorry, Anna. She just passed away."

"But she can't have," I objected. "I have to tell her about the concert." *They've made a mistake,* I thought. *Stupid women.*

I went to Oma and picked up her hand. The volunteer, a middle-aged woman from another barracks, tried to pull me away gently.

I turned to her. "She can't be dead! She's the only one . . . She's the only one who understands. My own mother thinks it's shameful somehow or something, you don't understand, she *can't be dead!* Oma! Wake up! Wake up!"

"Someone go get her mother," the woman said. I held on to Oma's hand. And I told her everything that had happened. How strong my voice was, how the director complimented me on my interpretation, how perfect it all was.

She had a little smile on her face, and for a while I imagined she could hear me.

I don't know how long I was there. Mother turned up, so did Aunt Mina. They both cried. I wouldn't cry. I was too angry. She really was dead. She had left me, and that wasn't fair.

Then I had another thought. She'd asked me, but I didn't listen. Now what would we bury her in? I hadn't packed her shroud.

Aunt Mina had a white nightgown. We dressed Oma in that with small white socks on her feet and one of Mother's scarves for her head. The funeral was the next morning. Rabbi Adler conducted the service. The rain poured down. We stood there, deep in mud. Klara was there too, and her mother and father and Rudi. In fact, there were lots of people there, although most weren't there to say good-bye to Oma. The men were allowed just one pass a week to visit their wives, but they could always get a pass to go to a funeral. With up to thirty people a day dying of starvation, cold, and disease, funerals quickly became the way for families to meet.

The rabbi said the Kaddish, the prayer for the dead, and then the thin wood casket was lowered into the ground. Mother held my hand, so did Aunt Mina. They were both crying. I was still too angry to cry. The casket was loosed from its rope. It made a horrible splashing sound as it sank, and then something truly grotesque happened—the casket began to float up because there was so much water in the grave. I screamed, turned, and fled.

❖ ❖ ❖

I still dream about it. That casket floating up toward me.

The next day in the office Rabbi Adler spoke to me.

"Anna, I've started a Torah study group for young people in the afternoons. I'd like it very much if you could attend."

"I don't know anything about that sort of thing," I said.

He smiled. "So you'll learn. A lot of young people have joined," he said. "It's better than doing nothing all day. How about it?"

"All right," I agreed. "I'll try." Anything to take my mind off Oma.

I arrived in a barracks that was filled with young people from the ages of about fourteen to twenty. Standing in the front was a middle-aged man with a beard. He introduced himself as Professor Malkovitch, and told us he had taught religion and philosophy at the university in Berlin, before he'd been fired because he was a Jew. He suggested that we begin at the beginning, studying Genesis.

He spoke for a while about the story of Genesis, when a young man with wild blond hair leaped up and interrupted him.

"Professor, if Eve hadn't eaten from the forbidden fruit, which God *warned* her not to eat, wouldn't the world still be a perfect place? Didn't she let in knowledge, and with that, the concept of good and evil?"

I scowled. It always ended up being the female who was at fault! Without stopping to think that I knew nothing and should keep my mouth shut, I burst out, "If God knows everything, don't you think he knew Eve would eat the apple? So He must have planned it that way." Everyone was staring at me. In a smaller voice I said, "It wasn't her fault, at all."

The young man shot back. "If she hadn't eaten that apple, that day, we wouldn't be *here*, right now."

Someone else piped up. "Are you saying this is all Eve's fault?"

"Yes," the young man insisted. "Without knowledge, we'd still be in a state of paradise."

"And maybe," said the professor, "there would then only be Adam and Eve in the world. After all, what use are people, an entire planet full, if only to live in a state of unconscious bliss? Only with knowledge can we become conscious. And this brings us to the heart of Genesis. Did God create a perfect world? And if not, why?"

"Professor, God created a world that needs to be completed. We must mend the world. *Tikkun Olam*. That is our job." The voice sounded familiar. I turned. It was Rudi speaking! "After all," he continued, "if the world were perfect, if we *knew* for sure God existed, we'd spend all our time praising him and doing nothing else. What else could you do if you knew, for *sure*, that there was a God? So God had to separate us from Him. He had to make a not-quite-perfect world for us to work on."

I was impressed. That was a really interesting way to think about things.

The young blond fellow yelled, "It's beyond mending. Evil has overtaken it. There is no good left!"

"We are still capable of choice, are we not?" asked Professor Malkovitch.

"What choice?" the blond-haired boy asked. "We can't decide if we'll live or die. It's not as if by working hard we can improve our lot. We have no choices left. The Nazis have taken them all away."

"We always have a choice," Rudi said.

"Like what?" the blond demanded, voice shrill.

"Love or hate," Rudi said. "Love or fear."

Everyone paused for a minute to think about that. Even the blond boy was silenced. Rudi caught my eye and winked at me. I shook my head at him, exasperated. I couldn't help but think of a line from Hamlet. "O what a rogue and peasant slave am I." Somehow Rudi just seemed such a rogue. Because for one split second I actually liked him. Which was amazing. I was used to despising him and I liked it that way. But what he said was really touching, really meant something.

I must say, I found that first session very interesting. So I started to go, regularly. It's odd. I hadn't been much of a Jew before the Nazis. Now I was learning all about it. And instead of hating my Jewishness for landing me in all that trouble, I began to discover so much to think about.

I stayed very busy that way for the next few months, working for Mother, practicing for concerts, and when I had time, going to Professor Malkovitch's classes.

One day when I returned to our barracks I found Mother waiting for me, a smile on her face.

It was the first real smile I'd seen on her since Oma had died.

"Close your eyes," she said.

"Why?"

"I have a surprise."

"A surprise?" I couldn't imagine. But I closed my eyes. She took my hand and led me into the barracks. We stopped. "Now, open them up." I opened them. There before me was a bed! A real bed! Off the floor.

"It's the Spanish refugees," Mother said. "They discovered where the barbed wire was stored and they helped themselves to some of it. They've figured out a way to remove the barbs and they've used the wire, crossing it in grids to build these cots." She lifted the straw sack to show me. "See? You and I will share. Aunt Mina can have one all to herself. We had to pay them, but it was worth it."

That night I slept off the floor for the first time in months and I actually went to sleep happy. But suddenly, in the middle of the night, a wire sprung loose on my side and I woke to find that my side of the cot had collapsed. I was stuck in a horrible V, my legs up in the air, my head in the air, my bottom resting on jutting wires. But Mother was asleep. And she was so exhausted I couldn't bring myself to wake her. So I stayed that way all night. When Mother woke up it took her a moment to realize what had happened. She scolded me terribly.

"You should have woken me."

Klara came along just then and saw my predicament. She began to laugh.

"Klara! Stop it. It isn't funny! Help get me out of here!"

"Anni," Mother scolded, "you're going to be so sore. Of course you should have woken me!"

Mother's side was on a separate grid so it hadn't affected her at all.

She and Klara tried to maneuver me out of the bed without my getting caught on a wire, while Aunt Mina and Mrs. Engel held down the edges, but everyone was laughing so hard they found it hard to accomplish anything.

When I was finally out, I was laughing so hard as well that I thought I wouldn't make it to the latrine in time, or, as we called them, the Châteaux. I grabbed Klara's hand and we ran. It had been so cold the last few nights that the mud had finally hardened so we were able to get there quickly. But what we found . . .

An older lady lay at the bottom of the ladder, dead, frozen.

"She must have fallen off the ladder," Klara said. "It was so cold last night. The ladder must have been like ice."

"And then she couldn't get up," I added. "So she lay here, alone, until she died."

"They should just shoot us now and get it over with!" Klara exclaimed.

"Don't say that," I admonished her. "Perhaps they're going to do just that!"

"I don't care! I don't care. At least it would be quick. What did that poor woman ever do to deserve this? What kind of God could allow such a thing? I hate Him! I hate Him!"

That afternoon I had another Torah class. I brought up what Klara had said.

"Professor," I asked, "do you think God watches over all of us, individually?"

"What do *you* think?" he asked, as usual, answering a question with another question.

"I don't know," I replied. "If He does, He isn't doing a good job. Maybe you can only believe in Him if you believe He's not really in charge. We are."

An Orthodox girl got up and said, "Oh, He's in charge all right! And this is a punishment for not keeping His laws. All Jews will be punished for those who strayed."

That created an uproar.

"I don't want anything to do with a God like that!" I declared.

"And do you really think you have a choice?" she demanded.

"God isn't like a mean parent, punishing you whenever you do something wrong!" I exclaimed. "God has to be better than that! More than that!"

"I think," Professor Malkovitch said, "that you are on your way to answering your own question, Miss Hirsch. If God is more, what is His role?"

"You know one of the reasons we have so much trouble seeing God as something other than a big powerful human?" a young woman piped up.

"What?" asked the professor.

"You keep calling God Him. Isn't there something else we could call Him? I mean, It? I mean . . . you know."

"We could call him Adonai. Would that make it easier to discuss?" the professor asked.

The young woman seemed satisfied. And the conversation

moved on to discuss the Book of Job. And why we suffer.

Still, despite what you called God—Him or It, or even Adonai—I was starting to agree with Klara. Something was *very* wrong, no matter what you called the all powerful one. After all, if Adonai was all powerful—*why* was this happening?

Six

Suit the action to the word, the word to the action.
—Shakespeare, *Hamlet*

I CAN HEAR FOOTSTEPS. Someone is coming near the woodpile. Klara squeezes my hand so hard I think she might break it. I hear voices. French. Not German. A dog barks. Someone is pulling at the wood. They must not know how to open it. Which must mean . . .

"Here! Here!" A man's voice, still French, not German. A dog barks frantically, near us. I think I might faint. Klara starts to cry. I turn to her.

"We aren't going to give up," I whisper fiercely. "You hold on to my hand. Don't let go, no matter what."

The dog is going crazy now. Howling. And then, the woodpile swings away. The light almost blinds me. It takes a minute before I can see. I look up. A French gendarme is staring at us, his dog barking wildly. He looks confused now that he's found us.

I pull Klara up. I shake out my legs. Klara seems paralyzed. I shove her a little and point to her legs. She follows my example as if sleepwalking, moving a little.

I smile at the gendarme as I look around, get my bearings. He raises his gun as if my smile is some kind of threat. Madame Debard rounds the corner of the house, with three of her own dogs. I see her say something to them. Her dogs immediately head for the gendarme's dog and attack him. Madame Debard is motioning to me, run, run. She points toward the trees, the woods just beyond. Klara's hand is still in mine. Madame Debard hurries over to us and begins to scream at the gendarme.

"Get your dog away! He'll hurt our dogs. Bad dog. Help me here!"

The gendarme can't concentrate on everything. We jump away from the dogs as if frightened. And then I grab Klara's hand even tighter, pull her, and we run.

"Hey!" the gendarme screams after us. I glance back. Guy is there now and has managed to trip in front of the gendarme so he can't chase us. I'm just glad I don't see any Gestapo. They'd have shot us by now.

And then, a shot whistles past my ear. Klara shrieks and falls. I kneel down. "Are you hit?"

"No! But they're shooting at us!"

"Get up!" I scream at her. "Our only chance is to run. Get up!!"

She scrambles up, and I pull her toward the trees. There is a manure pit with wooden planks over it just ahead of us, but I don't want to be a target up on the planks so I pull Klara around it. Many voices are screaming now. I look over my shoulder. I see two gendarmes running after us. But still no Gestapo. Klara and I are almost at the trees. More dogs are barking. Guy is running after the gendarmes, the dogs with him. Klara and I reach the trees. I look back. Two gendarmes are running across the planks. And then they aren't. They've fallen through the planks into the manure pit!

I pull Klara into the woods. We crash through the undergrowth and the trees, running so hard all I can hear is the blood throbbing in my ears. We are gasping for breath, crashing into tree branches, cutting our legs on sharp leaves, twigs, thistles. I don't care. I won't slow down.

Finally Klara jerks her hand out of mine and collapses on the forest floor. Her chest heaves so hard she can't even speak. Neither can I. I sink down beside her.

Finally, when I have enough air in my lungs to speak, I say, "Did you see?"

"What?"

"They fell into the manure pit!"

"No!"

"Yes!"

She actually starts to laugh.

"I don't think they'll be coming after us right away," I grin.

"Unless there were more than those two," she says. "There could have been. The others could have been searching the house or something."

It is almost dark. I try to think what we should do next. Should we try to find another farmhouse? Should we try to get to the village of Le Chambon, to Pastor Trocmé's house? Should we try to get to another town altogether? And then I have an idea.

"We need to get to another farmhouse," I tell Klara. "I think I know one not too far from here. I visited it once with Rudi. But it's on the other side of the Debards' farm. We'll have to go back, then circle around. Otherwise I'm sure to get us lost."

Klara doesn't argue. We have to do *something*. So we begin to go back, staying as far away from the farmhouse as possible. We walk quickly, but it gets darker and darker. I begin to worry. And I realize we aren't going to make it out of the woods before nightfall. The moon will rise and give us some light later, but now it is too low to be of any help.

"Klara," I say, "we'd better rest here until the moon comes up. Then we can try again."

We find a soft spot, covered with pine needles, and we rest up against a large tree. It's a warm night, at least. Not warm enough to be outside all night in comfort, but we won't freeze to death.

For a moment neither of us speaks.

"Close call," I say.

"Thank you," she says.

"What for?"

"Getting us out of there. I'd *never* have had the nerve."

It's a clear night, and before long the stars are shining and I can see the moon rising over the treetops.

"Ready?" I ask her.

"Ready."

Fortunately, we are quite close to the edge of the trees. I lead Klara out of the forest so that we are standing on a grazing meadow for sheep, rolling hills stretching out ahead of us. I can see the farmhouse we are heading for, lights blinking, in the distance. It will take us at least an hour to walk to it.

"We shouldn't talk," I say. "We don't want the dogs to hear us and start barking. Let's go."

It's amazing how well I know the area now. And lucky

for us too. I have to concentrate on keeping us going in the right direction, but I do well, and finally we arrive at the farmhouse. The dogs start to bark from the barn. One from the house barks. I knock on the door. An older man answers, white hair, bright blue eyes.

"Hello. Anna isn't it?"

"Yes. Hello, Monsieur Chave. This is my friend Klara. You see, we were hiding with Madame Debard, but we got discovered."

"Oh!" he exclaims. "Come in. Come in. Matilde. Come down!"

His wife appears and immediately fusses over us as if we were half-drowned cats. She heats us up some soup and makes us tea and puts blankets over our shoulders to warm us. Then she settles us into a double bed just off the kitchen, and tells us that we'll stay with them until this whole terrible business is over.

I cuddle under the quilt, warm and full. I turn to say something to Klara. But she's already fast asleep.

But I can't sleep. My blood is still racing. I'm worried about the others. Have the police caught any Jews? There are so many of us here. And what about Madame Debard and her family? Were they arrested for hiding us? I suppose I won't know until the morning. News travels fast here. Until then, I can only hope. And pray.

I remember when I first heard of Le Chambon-sur-Lignon. We'd been in Gurs for almost a year. It was September. I had just done a very difficult concert—some songs from *The Magic Flute* with the full orchestra. I had gone back to my barracks when Madame Lévy from OSE walked in. She was a lovely woman. OSE was one of the many relief organizations that had come to Gurs. In fact, I'd made up a song about them for the cabaret act we'd developed. You know, using all the initials. There were the Jewish ones: OSE was the Jewish child welfare organization; ORT specialized in job training and had set up sewing workshops in the camp; HICEM was an organization that helped people to emigrate; JDC was the American Joint Distribution Committee. And of course, there was CIMADE and the Quakers and the Swiss Red Cross. How did that song go? Oh, I can't remember. But, anyway, there was Madame Lévy from OSE asking Mother whether she'd like to get me out of the camp. Without a moment's hesitation Mother said yes. She never let me consider the idea of staying with her and Aunt Mina.

At that point in the war, September of 1941, the Vichy government had decreed that "no foreigner of the Israelite race will hence forth be freed from lodging or internment centers if he did not live in France before May 10, 1940." That meant that even if we could find someone to live with, the French government was going to keep us prisoners—all to please the German masters and the Frenchmen in power who hated the Jews. People were still allowed to emigrate, though—*if* any country would take them. Still, some women and children were allowed to go stay in other supervised centers, as long as the government knew where they were. Apparently, the Swiss Red Cross had opened some children's homes in Le Chambon-sur-Lignon, a small village in the Haute-Loire region of France not far from Vichy to the northwest, Lyon to the northeast. All this was explained to Mother and to me. Klara, Rudi, and four others were to go. One was the blond young man from the Torah class named Peter. Another was Mordechai, who was fourteen and Orthodox. And there were two girls, Lotti and Monique, both born in France but to parents who had emigrated from Poland.

Within two days it was all arranged. It happened so fast. I remember saying good-bye at the outskirts of the camp. It was early morning. There was a thick fog. The barrier to the outer road had been lifted, and all the families came to say good-bye. There was no guard there.

I whispered to Mother, "Run. You could just run now. Why not leave?"

"I can't, Anni," she said. "I have too many people to take care of. What would they do without me?"

"Aunt Mina?" I said.

"Then who will stay with your mother?" Aunt Mina said, smiling gently at me.

"Should I stay?" I asked, suddenly sure I was doing the wrong thing. How could I desert them?

"No!" Aunt Mina said fiercely.

"No!" Mother echoed. "Anywhere is better than here."

I kissed them then, and hugged them.

"Anni," Mother said.

"Yes?"

"I think you are very talented."

"Really?"

"I'm sorry it took a war for me to realize. . . ."

"You were just trying to protect me," I said.

"I didn't do a very good job," she answered.

"It's not your fault." And I gave her a million kisses and Aunt Mina too, until they were both laughing.

" 'Parting is such sweet sorrow,' " I quoted. " 'That I shall say good night till it be morrow.' "

"No last joke?" Aunt Mina asked.

I racked my brain. "I have one. A woman who speaks with a thick Yiddish accent goes into a fancy restaurant.

" 'We don't serve Jews here,' the manager declares.

" 'Dat's all right,' she replies. 'I don't eat 'em.' "

Aunt Mina laughed. She always laughed at my jokes. And that time even Mother smiled.

"Promise me," Mother called after me, "that you'll be all right. Promise me."

"I promise," I said. We boarded a regular bus, just like regular people, to the train station and then took the train to Toulouse. I remember we passed the cathedral at Lourdes on the way. The sun was rising and its rays bathed the golden dome, illuminating it so that it looked like something out of a fairy tale. I'd forgotten that physical beauty could exist. I hadn't forgotten about other beauty—I saw that daily in my rehearsals, great artists creating beauty all the time, but to see something like that—it took my breath away.

And then Madame Lévy took us to dinner in Toulouse. We had chicken soup with milk in it, the first decent meal I'd eaten in a year.

We got back on the train and went to Lyon where we stayed in a real hotel for a few hours. Rudi continued to make a pest of himself, flopping on my bed and saying very rude things. From Lyon we took a train to St. Étienne and from there we changed to a small little train, which took us up to Le Chambon. We arrived there in the early evening. By then I was so exhilarated—I was really, truly out of the camp. And I was both pleased and horrified to see that life was continuing. Perhaps not a normal life, but people worked and ate, even laughed. I was pleased about that. What horrified me was that I knew most of the people we'd seen on our way to Le Chambon had no idea what was going on in Gurs and in other camps like Gurs. And I guess they didn't *want* to know because maybe then they'd have to do something. Maybe then they'd realize that collaborating with the Germans wasn't the right thing to do, that the whole country should fight! I'll bet a million francs that if Hitler had invaded England *they* wouldn't have collaborated. Not Mr. Churchill.

We were taken directly to our new home. It was a small house atop a hill, at the edge of a wood, a meadow beneath us. The view of the town was obstructed by more woods further down the hill, so it was like our own little world. The seven of us looked at each other and then we began to whoop and scream and leap around. We were free! Free! I sucked in the fresh fragrant air, I raised my arms up and began to sing, and to dance a hora I'd been taught in the camp. We all joined hands and we whirled around and around. Soon the other young people from the house—about fifteen of them—were standing outside staring at us. Within minutes they were clapping. The circle got bigger as more and more of them joined in, and we were all dancing and singing as the sun set, and for that moment I forgot everything and was perfectly happy.

SEVEN

To be, or not to be: that is the question.
—Shakespeare, *Hamlet*

MY FIRST MORNING IN Le Chambon was marked by sunlight. In Gurs every morning we awoke to the dark windowless barracks, and to the reek of the Châteaux. But that morning, light, so bright it hurt my eyes, streamed through the windows. A cock crowed. The smells were exquisite—fresh mountain air coming in through the open window, mingled with the odor of food cooking in the kitchen. We raced downstairs. There we were met by Paul Hébert. He was in charge of the home run by the Swiss Red Cross, and I could see right away that he was determined to take care of us. He couldn't have been more than twenty-five or so and yet, here he was, a young, very handsome man I might add, with large gray eyes and thick black hair, behaving as if he were a mother hen.

"Look at you," he clucked. "We'll have to get some food into you." We were either rail thin or bloated with water but none of us was healthy.

"Now, we don't have much, but you must eat." And he gave us a kind of porridge soup and toast and even some goat's milk. This wasn't the first time we'd been fed by the

Swiss Red Cross either. In Gurs they had set up a food station for children but there were so many of us that each group got to go only every few weeks. They fed us Ovaltine and some chocolate. It probably kept us from actually starving to death.

"Eat!" he ordered. "Eat."

We did. We gobbled up all we could, but we were used to so little that we couldn't finish the food on our plates.

Klara came up with a wonderful idea. She held up her piece of bread. "If we toasted this," she said, "it would be like a cracker. We could toast our leftover bread and send it in packages to our families in Gurs."

"You're a genius," I said admiringly.

"Takes after her older brother." Rudi grinned.

"You'd be lucky to have half her brains," Peter said to Rudi, gazing at Klara.

"Well," said Rudi, "thank you *very* much!"

The way Peter was looking at Klara made it obvious that he wasn't *all* prickles and barbs. He had a soft spot deep inside, and Klara had seemingly touched it.

After breakfast the young people staying in the house walked down to the village together. Rudi and Klara went with about half of the others to the Cévenole School, the school for advanced study, grade eight and up. I had to go to the public school with Peter and a few others.

In Mannheim, Jewish children were thrown out of public school in 1935. But the Jewish community made their own school, staffed by Jewish teachers who had been fired from their jobs. The school had only gone up to the eighth grade, though, and after that I'd had no more classes. Rudi and Klara had been tutored at home—which included French. That's why they were advanced enough to go to the Cévenole School and I wasn't.

Peter grumbled all the way there. "What good is it to send us to school?" he complained. "The Nazis will be here soon, and they'll catch us or shoot us. We should be training to fight. They should teach us how to shoot, not how to read and speak French." Peter was also from Germany. I don't think he'd had any family in Gurs. I wondered if he was so bitter because something terrible had happened to his family back in Germany. I felt I couldn't ask him though. Instead, I tried to cheer him up.

"You should learn the language," I said to him, assessing his mass of blond hair, his blue eyes, his high cheekbones. "With your looks, you could be on the stage. In fact, you could be a matinee idol."

"Don't get any ideas, Anna," he warned me. "My interests are elsewhere."

"Really, Peter," I retorted, quite insulted. "I'm not the *least* bit interested in you that way, believe me! I just know the theater. And I'm telling you, you'd be a natural."

Well, it *did* stop his whining. I think he even puffed up a bit, like a proud peacock.

At the public school the principal met us and had a brief chat with each of us in French. Then he directed everyone to different classrooms. I walked into mine, then stopped and looked around in confusion. The teacher, an older lady with gray hair and spectacles (type cast, I was thinking) said, "Come in, come in. Don't stand there sucking in air."

She spoke to me in a heavily French-accented German.

"No. There must be some mistake," I said. I was the only person sent to this class, I was sure I should have been sent elsewhere with some of the others.

"There is no mistake, my dear. This must be where the principal wants you. Fourth grade."

The little children were all giggling madly.

"You may sit on the bench back there."

What can I say? The bench was built for a nine-year-old child. And I was big, even for my age. My legs wouldn't fit under the desk and I had to stick them out in the aisle, and even then they bumped into another desk across the aisle. My desk mate was a little brown-eyed, brown-haired devil named Colette. She pounced on every mistake I made and encouraged the others to keep teasing me. So, I put my hands behind my head and slowly leaned back. The desk leaned with me. We began to tilt dangerously. Colette let out a shriek. I sat up and the desk returned to the ground with a thud. I grinned at Colette. She stared at me, then turned to the other students and told them *not* to laugh, it wasn't nice. And from then on, I had no problems with my classmates.

After school that day, we all met at the bottom of the hill. Paul was there waiting for us. "Before we go back to the house," he said, "I have a favor to ask. The Swiss Red Cross has three houses here in Le Chambon. One of them was given to us by a woman who owns a farm just down the road here. She needs help and, I hope you don't mind, I volunteered your services." Then he winked. None of us knew what the wink meant but we couldn't refuse. Well, Peter did manage to say something about slave labor but the rest of us were willing to help. We got to the farm and the woman greeted us. "You'll all get some at the end of the day," she said. "So please don't eat while you work."

By then, I was curious. What were we harvesting? She led us down a small path and there, in front of us, were fruit trees heavy with apples and plums. I thought that perhaps I'd died and gone to heaven. She explained that she had planted the trees to convince the people in the area that fruit *could* grow in such a high altitude. She smiled proudly. "As you can see, my little experiment has worked very well."

We were each given baskets. We moved into the grove and began to pick. As soon as my basket was full I climbed up an apple tree, perched on one of the limbs, pulled an apple off, smelled it, rolled it in my hands for a minute, and bit into it. Juice rolled down my chin. I stayed there for an hour, eating.

"You come down from there this instant!" Klara yelled when she finally found me. "You're going to be sick as a dog."

"No, I won't!" I said. And I wasn't. *She* was. And that was from eating the one apple she was given as a treat for all her work. I don't suppose there is any justice in this world.

At any rate, we settled into a routine very quickly. We'd go to school, do homework, do chores around the house and at night we'd sit outside, on a small balcony, and look at the stars, and we'd talk about all sorts of things. Although often it was about God.

Peter always started by saying something like: "The

human race is just a big fat mistake. You know, evolution that went wrong."

"Don't you believe in God at all?" Lottie asked.

"No."

"But," Rudi said, "just because you don't believe in God, that doesn't mean you have an excuse to give up on everything. If there is only us in this universe all the more reason to make moral choices."

Where did Rudi get off talking like this? "I think all that schooling is going to your head, Rudi," I said.

"Jealous?"

"No! I'm in grade six," I said, trying to be proud of it, trying not to blush in embarrassment. "Two grades in one month. So there."

"Excuse us," said Peter, "but we were trying to have a discussion here."

"Maybe," Klara said, "God does have a plan for all of us. And our challenge is to discover what the plan is."

Peter looked at her askance. "And was his plan for my father to be murdered in the street during Kristallnacht, because he was a Jew?"

Klara turned bright red.

"No," she said softly. "I suppose not."

For a little while, none of us spoke. But Peter looked so miserable that I said something just so he wouldn't feel everyone was staring at him.

"Perhaps," I said, "God is unknowable. That's what I got out of our sessions with Professor Malkovitch. God is there but in such a mysterious way that we'll never really understand it. So, basically, it's like Peter said, we're on our

own, and, like Rudi said, we have to make our own decisions. We have to choose between good and evil. On the
other hand there is a higher power, and that power, maybe,
is the source of love."

"Oh!" said Peter sarcastically, "that sounds very pretty.
You mean if you make the right choice you'll go to heaven?"

"No, I mean you will pay a price, inside, for the wrong
choices."

"Those Gestapo goons looked *perfectly* happy to me,"
Peter said.

"They *think* they are," I countered. "But they don't know
the real happiness of behaving with goodness. Theirs is a
little world. Look at Pastor Trocmé. His soul is huge. He is
connected with the goodness of the universe."

That shut Peter up. He knew exactly what I meant. We
had an example of someone with a big soul right in front of
us. Pastor Trocmé was one of the pastors of Le Chambon,
and he preached openly against collaborating with the
Nazis. He encouraged everyone to help *anyone* that was in
need, and he was not the only example—there was also his
wife, their children, and Pastor Theis, the other pastor of
Le Chambon, who preached and worked just as diligently
as Pastor Trocmé. Pastor Theis was also the head of the
Cévenole School. And, of course, there were all the others
of Le Chambon who were taking care of us. Still, after a
few minutes Peter said quietly, into the silence, "Why are
there so few like them?"

At that Klara put her hand on his. Rudi said softly,
"Remember what Father always told us, Klara?"

"About the angels?" Klara replied.

"The soul of man was created on the first day; angels on the second," Rudi said, as if repeating something he'd heard a million times. "If people keep the spirit of God dominant within them they are told: 'You are greater than the angels.'"

We all stared into the sky filled with stars, and I thought about what *my* father used to say. That we are all shards of light and that in each of us is a spark of the divine.

Not long after that, at the beginning of November, the first snow fell. Everything looked so clean. The snow sparkled in the sun. And by December there was so much snow that on days when it was packed just right we'd sled down the hill to school. That had been Rudi's idea, naturally. He dared me the first time. So, of course, I had to do it.

One morning after a particularly heavy snow we got on the sleds. This time Rudi was on the lead sled, lying face forward, his legs hooked onto the sled behind him. I lay on that one, my legs hooked onto the sled behind me—Klara, Lottie, and Monique sat upright on that one. We often made little trains.

The morning was crisp and clear, our breath froze as it came out of our mouths. Down we went, faster and faster. Rudi was outdoing himself. We were all screaming and yelling, my hair was whipping around into my face, my cheeks burning from the wind, when an even louder scream seemed to overtake ours. Eventually, we all heard it, and one by one we became quiet. And then, at the same moment, we realized what it was—the train. The train whistle. And we were heading straight for the tracks! We were going so fast that we couldn't fall off onto the snow unless we all did it together, and the train whistle was so loud we couldn't hear each other. The train was early, it shouldn't have been there, but it was. Some of the others, Hannah and Peter, who had walked were on the other side of the tracks, gesturing at us to stop, and screaming something.

I looked ahead at Rudi. He was hunched forward and obviously had no intention of stopping. As we reached the tracks the train chugged toward us, sparks flew as our sled crossed the rails, the train whistle blasted and, somehow, we made it. The sleds finally slowed down and we all tumbled off. Breathless, I said, "Rudi, we almost got killed!"

"Yes," he grinned, "but now we're all going to be very wide awake for our classes, aren't we?"

That night I realized that Rudi wasn't home in time for dinner, again. I'd noticed that he almost never ate with us anymore. I decided to watch for him so I could have a word when he got back. I hoped he wasn't making trouble for anyone in town. He could be such a nuisance.

I kept looking out our window until I spotted him coming, then I raced out into the corridor and ambushed him.

"Rudi!" I began.

"Hey, legs," he said, "are the grade-six kids giving you a hard time? If they are, you just tell me and I'll let them have it!"

"Very funny, Rudi. And by the way, it's grade seven now. What are you up to anyway?" I asked. "Not that I care. But Klara has enough to deal with without worrying about you."

"What am I up to? Well, let's see. It could have something to do with the fact that this village is *full* of Jews and most of them need to get to Switzerland, but none of them have papers."

"So?"

"So, forgery just happens to be one of my little specialties."

"What? You're joking, right?"

"No. *This* is a joke. One German Jew says to another, 'Can I borrow a cigarette paper?' The other replies 'No, I just used my last one to wrap my meat ration!'"

"Ha. Ha. You're just too funny," I said, trying very hard not to laugh. He *had* set that one up surprisingly well.

"Anyway," he continued, "I got to talking to some of the boys at school, and I found out that the resistance has ways to get Jews to Switzerland. But they need false papers. I learned how to make them while I was still in Germany."

"Really?" I said. I was truly thunderstruck. This clown, Rudi, had been doing work like that?

"Really. My tutor was an expert in calligraphy and he used to make me copy handwriting and do fancy pen work for hours at a time. I used to complain to Father that unless he wanted me to become a master forger it was a complete waste of time. Funny, huh?" He looked at me sharply as if something had just occurred to him. "You know, I could use some help at night delivering the papers to the different houses where Jews are waiting. Want to come along?"

"Is *that* a joke?"

"No. This is a joke. One Jew says—"

"Never mind," I said, giving him a light swat on the arm. "Of course I'll help."

"Good. After school I go to a small farm just outside of town. That's where all the equipment is set up. I'll tell you where it is, and if you meet me there around seven we can get twice as much done."

So I did. The first night I took papers to a family of French Jews that had come here quite legally, afraid that the French government would eventually go after them the way they'd gone after the foreign Jews. They were the smart ones, of course, because it was obvious that no Jew was really safe anywhere in France. The next night it was a family from Poland, the next a young man from Russia. Then, a young couple from Germany, and after that a woman all alone from Paris. But it wasn't only Jews who needed to escape. There were the political types too: socialists, communists, and men who wanted to join DeGaulle as freedom fighters. And, there was the resistance. Somehow Rudi was connected with them. In fact, some of them lived in a hotel in town, and he made them false papers too. The blank forms he needed from City Hall used to appear on his desk when he needed them—everyone in the town seemed to find a quiet way to help.

The amazing thing was that refugees were staying all over Le Chambon and the surrounding area, and the inhabitants just took them in as if it were the normal thing to do. The refugees would get off the noon train or arrive by bus. Some would find their way to the café or to the hotel and ask where they might go, who might take them in. Sometimes they'd have a friend or a cousin who would meet them and already have a place for them to hide. Sometimes they would just knock on the first house that looked friendly and ask for help. No one was turned away. Somehow everyone found refuge. Some stayed in the same place for months, others for only a few days before moving from place to place, others tried to arrange to flee to Switzerland.

One night, Rudi came with me on a delivery. We had to go to a farm far away from the village and he needed to show me the way.

"How did all these refugees end up here?" I asked him as we walked, realizing that I'd just taken it for granted since I'd been there.

"I'm not sure," he replied. "But it's a resort in the summer so I think some were used to coming here. Others found their way here by accident. Some, like us, have been sent here. The Quakers have been very busy getting children out of the camps and from what I can gather they had the first arrangement with Pastor Trocmé."

"Is it true," I asked, "that Pastor Trocmé and Pastor Theis are pacifists? That they don't believe in fighting at all?"

"Yes." Rudi laughed. "They were in trouble before the war for preaching that France shouldn't fight Germany. Now they're in trouble for preaching that France shouldn't collaborate with the Germans."

"Aren't they in danger? Aren't the Vichy authorities aware of what they are preaching?"

Rudi shrugged. "The authorities must be aware of it. But so far, they seem to have left them alone. You know most of the people in this area are Protestant—Huguenots. Hundreds of years ago, as a minority in France, they were persecuted terribly by the majority, the Catholics. Their churches were burned, the men were sent off in slave galleys, the women were imprisoned in dungeons. They know all about persecution. They remember."

"Do you mean to tell me we have the Catholics to thank for our safe haven here?"

"No, the Protestants. Although there are some Catholics in this area that are helping."

"Stupid, that's not what I mean."

"You mean—you mean if the Catholics hadn't persecuted the Huguenots, the Huguenots wouldn't have learned to empathize with the persecuted, and we'd have nowhere to go?"

"Maybe," I said. "Although," I added, "I'm sure it's not *only* that. With so many people helping there must be lots of different reasons."

"I've asked some of them," Rudi replies. "You know what they say? But of course we help—what else could we do? As if it never occurred to them *not* to. It's the right thing and that's that." He pauses. "Your little idea is too simple—and it's disgusting too."

"Is it?" I replied. "It means that Huguenots learned something from their suffering. It wasn't in vain."

"So just take that a step further. Then their suffering was actually good. Maybe all this persecution will be good for the Jews!"

"That's not at all—you're twisting it!"

"No, I'm not. That's the logical conclusion of what you're saying. You probably think it's all part of some great plan by God. But I think it stinks."

"Rudi," I said, "that's not what I mean. You have to admit that unless these people, the Huguenots, learned from their suffering, that their suffering would have been useless." And then, I remembered an idea that Professor Malkovitch had told us. "Maybe that's how God *has* made a perfect world, Rudi—he's made us capable of learning. We are created to learn, and to *try* to become perfect."

"Try is right," Rudi said. "Try and get nowhere."

"But if we succeeded—if we became perfect—what would be the point?" I grinned at him. "Well, that's one thing *you* don't have to worry about anyway!"

I guess that remark was *not*, as they say in the theater, perfect timing. Because it was mild that day, mild enough that the sun had thawed the snow just enough for it to be perfect for snowballs. Rudi crouched down, patted a big fat one into shape, slowly rose to his feet, and took aim. "Who's not perfect? Come on," he demanded. "Say it. I'm *perfect!*"

But I wouldn't. I *wouldn't!* Give in to Rudi? *Never!*

"Rudi," I warned. "Don't. You'll be sorry." I started to back away.

Whap! The snowball hit me square in the face. Quickly I wiped it away, bent down, made one myself, and threw. Hit him right on his neck. I could see it dripping under his shirt and into his jacket. I grinned.

He got a look on his face, though, that I didn't like, and he wasn't bending down for another snowball. Instead, suddenly he was running straight for me and before I could move he'd tackled me to the ground. He picked up a huge handful of snow and mashed it into my face. I grabbed a handful myself and, since he was practically on top of me, I reached around and mushed it into his neck. "Ahhh!" he screamed. Then we started rolling around in the snow, throwing it on each other, pushing it in each other's face, until our faces were burning from cold and we were laughing so hard we could hardly catch our breath. We had managed to soak each other to the skin.

Rudi finally offered his hand and began to help me up. I kicked his legs out from under him and he landed flat on his back. "Give up?" I said, hands on hips.

"I give up," he sighed. And then a look of panic came over him. "The papers!" he exclaimed. He drew them out of his pocket. They were soaked through. He glared at me.

"*You* started it," I reminded him, "so don't go blaming me."

He muttered something that I couldn't catch, which was probably just as well. He turned back to the village. "We'll have to dry them out," he said. When we got back we dried them in front of the fire, then I ironed them. We started our walk all over again, except this time we were both tired and grumpy. Instead of talking about God we spent the entire trip blaming each other for getting the papers wet. By the time the night was over we weren't even talking to each other. The idiot!

EIGHT

When sorrows come, they come not single spies,
But in battalions.
—Shakespeare, *Hamlet*

BY AUGUST WE'D BEEN in Le Chambon almost a year. It's funny the way time flew by—in May I had been admitted to the Cévenole School. And, of course, at night I delivered papers, and read and read and read. It was *very* demanding, the homework, the reading. And I hated math. I couldn't understand it. Rudi, of course, was a genius at it. He did help me when we got back from our deliveries—but he'd get irritated with me for not catching on, so I'd dare him to recite the passage from Molière he was studying. Naturally, he couldn't. We enjoyed tormenting each other.

I had managed to organize a little theatrical night in our house—a kind of talent night where once a month people got to do an act. I did something different each time—one time I'd sing, another I'd do a cabaret comedy act, another I'd get some kids and we'd do a scene from a play. It was a lot of fun, despite Rudi's constant teasing about it.

I had many letters from Mother and Aunt Mina. They kept saying that they were fine, but in July, Klara got a letter from her mother saying that Mother was, in fact, quite ill and weak, and at the same time I got a letter from Mother saying that Klara's father was very ill. We fretted and worried about it until I approached Madame Lévy, who still came to Le Chambon occasionally with children, and asked her to get me permission to return to Gurs to visit my mother. Why not? I was legally staying in the Red Cross house, I didn't need false papers. Why shouldn't I be able to visit? The others were sure I'd never get permission, but somehow the Swiss Red Cross arranged it all for me. One day, our house leader, Paul, came and told me that I would go the next day by train to Gurs. I think this made everyone else feel terrible that they hadn't tried, but I assured them that after my visit, one by one, they could try to go, too.

I had to go down to the stream to bathe because the water pump had gone completely dry in the house. Still it was wonderful to dunk myself in that cold, clear spring water, to dress in clothes I'd boiled clean, to get myself all ready. Everyone gave me letters to take and somehow Rudi managed to get six tins of sardines, which I packed in my leather briefcase. Paul wasn't able to go with me, so I had to travel alone. But I was almost sixteen and I felt I was up to it.

"You'll watch for your stops now, won't you?" Klara fussed.

"Of course I will."

"Well, you know how you daydream. Your mind wanders. And suddenly you'll be past your stop and your ticket won't hold."

"Don't worry! I'll watch."

"Try not to draw *too* much attention to yourself, legs,"

Rudi said. "No loud humming, singing, entertaining the train with jokes. You might be tempted to go on a talent search. Bring all those singing grandmas back to Le Chambon with you."

"Honestly!" I said. "You two are worse than my mother."

I spent the train trip retracing the exact route we'd taken a year ago, and inspired by Rudi's admonitions, trying out my jokes—in my own head, for once. I had decided to do a series of rabbi jokes for the next concert, and rehearsing them kept me from worrying.

I got off the bus at Gurs just before dark, but the guards wouldn't let me in. I showed my papers and my permission slips, but they muttered something about the camp being closed. I was so disappointed I almost cried. But I didn't. I waited for the last bus and took it to the small town of Gurs, right near the camp. I walked into the first inn I saw and asked the little white-haired lady if I could stay there. She agreed if I'd help with the evening meal—there was no running water and someone needed to carry it from the well on the main street. I had a little money, which was enough for them, as long as I helped out. That night I tumbled into bed exhausted but woke up before dawn. I caught the first bus to Gurs, but again I wasn't allowed in. This time, since it wasn't dark, I walked along the barbed wire and called out to the first woman I saw, "Can you find Sarah Hirsch? She's my mother. I've come to visit her, but they won't let me in!"

"Yes! Yes!" The woman knew my mother, everyone did. I heard her shouting, "Sarah Hirsch's daughter is here! Get Sarah! Her daughter is here!"

I had to wait at least thirty minutes before I saw my mother walking slowly toward me. Her thick black hair had turned completely gray, so at first I didn't recognize her. She was stooped and thin. For a moment my voice caught in my throat and I couldn't speak.

"Mommy?"

"Anni! Look at you! Such a beautiful young lady." And she started to cry.

"Don't cry, Mommy. Don't cry. Why can't I get in to see you? What's happening?"

Mother came as close to the wire as she could. I did too. We couldn't touch because it was a double-wire fence, but at least we didn't have to shout.

"I'm quite sure that we are about to be transported east," Mother said. "To Poland, perhaps."

"No! They can't. The French wouldn't! Why?"

"Why, I can't answer. I suppose because they want to please Hitler and delivering Jews to him is a good way to do that."

For a moment I felt I would go mad. I had so many emotions coursing through me I could hardly stand up. My knees grew weak and I almost toppled over.

"Anni!" Mother said. "Promise me you'll be all right. Don't allow yourself to be defeated. Remember—*they* can't defeat us. We can only defeat ourselves."

I didn't know what she meant really. *Hadn't* they defeated us? But, from the tone of her voice, I knew that I had to at least appear strong for her. She didn't need to worry about me. So I straightened my shoulders and fought back the tears and waited to speak until my voice was strong.

"I promise, Mother," I said.

Aunt Mina came running up then, followed by Mrs. Engel. "Anni! Anni!" They were all calling my name. "How are you? How are the others? How are Klara and Rudi? What is life like in Le Chambon?" I tried to answer all the questions, and I stayed there for at least two hours. Finally, I could see Mother was too exhausted to stand anymore. I threw the tins of sardines over the fence, along with the letters, which I'd wrapped around the sardines. At least there was no mud for them to fall in—the ground was caked and dry. I told them I'd be back the next day at the same time. We said good-bye, Mother blowing me a kiss.

As they left I called softly after Aunt Mina. She came back to the fence.

"What's wrong with Mother?"

"She's developed boils, sweetheart. She's got horrible sores on her back and they've had to lance them in the hospital. She's had a lot of pain." Aunt Mina's eyes filled with tears. "Why didn't we run when we had the chance?" she said bitterly.

"Because," I said, "you were both thinking of others— Mother about everyone here, you about Mother."

Aunt Mina nodded. "Thank God you were able to come, Anni," she said. "Thank God."

I wasn't sure I wanted to thank God for anything.

Every morning I went to visit Mother. Every morning I was turned away at the gate and had to visit through the barbed wire. I had arrived there August 2. On August 5, Mother told me that they were being taken to the station the next morning. I asked her to fetch Madame Lévy and when she came to the fence, I pleaded with her to get me permission from the authorities so I could go to the station. Later that day she got a message to me in Gurs that she'd obtained permission for me and that I was to go to the station at Oloron-Sainte-Marie. I said good-bye to my hosts, trading them my ration stamps for bread I could give Mother, and took the bus into Oloron. There was nowhere for me to stay there, my money was gone, so I slept under a tree on a street near the station.

Some time, near daybreak, I awoke to find two French gendarmes standing over me.

"What do you think you're doing?" A small kick in the leg got me talking.

"I'm waiting to go to the station in the morning," I replied, breaking out into a cold sweat.

"Oh, are you? Maybe you're waiting for a man to come along who has money to offer you—for favors."

"I'm not!"

"Let's get a look at her," one said, a big hulking middle-aged man. "If she's pretty, we'll take her to the hotel."

The other shone his flashlight in my face. Quickly I pushed my hair over my brows and grimaced so as to look as ugly as possible.

"I could shut my eyes," said the other one, a younger fellow, but also very heavyset. *They* were getting food from somewhere.

"Yes," said the other, "nothing wrong with shutting your eyes."

My knapsack was beside me. Slowly I put my hand on the straps until I had a good grip on it. They were both so fat that I figured they wouldn't be able to reach down quickly to grab me. So staying low, I scrambled along the ground, scraping and cutting my knees but oblivious to the pain, at the time. Once out of their reach I got up and ran. They ran a few steps and I heard one of them say, "Forget it, she was ugly anyway."

I kept running until I reached the train station. When I got there, I saw, to my horror, that the trains were on the tracks and they were already full of people. But they weren't passenger trains. They were *cattle* cars. They'd put all those people in cattle cars. For a moment I thought I was going to be sick, but my stomach was too empty even for that.

Another gendarme came up to me as I was doubled over near the tracks.

"Young lady, are you sick?"

He called me young lady. I looked up at him in surprise. "No, no, I'm fine. I'm just upset. I have permission to visit my mother, but how will I find her?"

"What barracks was she in?" he asked.

"M."

"We'll find her," he said, and he gave me an encouraging smile. "You wait here."

He was back around ten minutes later. "Follow me."

"Thank you," I said. "Thank you so much."

"This is tearing me apart," he confided to me as we walked. "It's a day I thought I'd never see. I'm ashamed to be a Frenchman. Here's your mother's car. Let me help you up."

He hoisted me into the car. Mother saw me immediately and threw herself on me. We held each other tight for so long, I don't know how long. And Aunt Mina clung on to both of us.

I brought out my bread and gave it to them, and they tried to share it with everyone—so it ended up being just a few bites each.

"Do you have a joke for me?" Aunt Mina asked.

"Of course I do," I said. "Let's see." I paused for effect. "Moses Montefiore, a great Jewish man of charity in the 1800s, once went to a dinner party. But he was seated next to an anti-Semitic nobleman.

"'I have just come back from a trip to Japan,' said the nobleman, 'and I found it to be a very unusual country. Do you know it has neither pigs nor Jews?'

"'Well then,' Montefiore replied, 'you and I should go there, so it will have a sample of each.'"

Aunt Mina laughed. Others in the crowd began to listen. So I told the jokes I'd been practicing on the train.

"A Hasid comes to see his rabbi. 'Rabbi,' he says, 'last night I had the most amazing dream! I dreamed that I was the leader of a thousand Hasidim.' The rabbi replies: 'Come back when a thousand Hasidim dream that you are their leader.'"

Of course Aunt Mina laughed again. So did many of the others.

"A rabbi suffers a heart attack and has to stay in the hospital for a few weeks. Naturally, one of his first visitors is the president of his synagogue. 'Rabbi,' he says, 'I want you to know that last night the board of directors voted on a resolution wishing you a quick recovery. And it passed, twelve to nine!'"

That got a bigger laugh.

"Then of course there is the one about two Jews who are bragging about their respective rabbis.

" 'My rabbi is such a genius, he can talk for an hour on any topic.'

" 'Hah!' said the other. 'My rabbi is such a genius he can talk for two hours on no topic at all!' "

"Sing us a song, Anni," Mother asked. I looked at her in surprise. She'd never asked me to sing before.

I sang a Hebrew prayer I'd learned while I was still in the camp.

> Grant peace to our world, goodness and blessing,
> mercy and compassion, life and love. Inspire us to
> banish forever hatred, war, and bloodshed. Help us to
> establish forever one human family doing Your Will
> in love and peace. O God of peace, bless us with peace.

When I'd finished there wasn't a sound in the car.

"Thank you," Mother said.

"Where is Mrs. Engel?" I asked.

"She managed to get into the car with Mr. Engel," Mother replied. "One over."

"I'll just go see her," I said, "and I'll be right back."

I jumped down from the car and ran over to the other one. Mrs. Engel was so happy to see me and sent her love over and over to her children. I was on my way back to Mother's car when a gendarme stopped me.

"Just where do you think you're going?"

"I have permission," I explain. "I'm visiting my mother."

"We'll see about that!" He grabbed the collar of my blouse and dragged me along the track to the platform where he presented me to his superior. The officer looked at my papers. He stared at me for a moment. "All right," he said. "But you stay at your mother's car."

I nodded. My mouth had gone dry. I realized how easy it would be for them to throw me into the car with the others. Who could stop them? I hurried to Mother's car, but now I was afraid to go back inside. What if the doors were suddenly closed, with me still inside? So I told Mother what had happened, and I stayed on the ground.

"Anna," Mother called to me, "I'll never see you again." She'd used my name. Not the baby version.

"Mother!"

"No, it's true. You know how Hitler hates the Jews. Why would he want us back? To resettle us as we're being told? Nonsense."

That was Mother. Always the realist.

"So you must promise me."

"What?"

"That you'll stay safe there in Le Chambon, and when this is all over you'll find Ilse and Max and you'll be a family, in America. Promise me."

"I promise, Mommy." I was trying not to cry, but tears were rolling down my cheeks. "But maybe," I said, "it'll never be over. Maybe Hitler will win."

"He won't," Mother said. "He won't. The Americans will come. You'll see."

And then there was a horrible commotion, as the French gendarmes ran to each car and pulled the doors closed and with a horrible, horrible clang, sealed them shut as if there were animals inside. Animals!

"Mommy! Aunt Mina!" I cried, but my cries were drowned out in the wail coming from inside the cars.

The gendarme who'd been kind to me was there, and he gently pulled me away and guided me to the platform for passenger trains. He found another woman who was waiting for the same train as me and he asked her if she'd see me on safely. She held my arm until our train pulled in, and then she found me a seat.

"Will you be all right?" she asked.

How could I be?

Would you be all right, I felt like screaming, if you'd just watched your family taken away, watched your entire *town* taken away, to be *murdered*. I'll never be all right.

Instead, I nodded. She patted my hand and went to find her own seat.

NINE

What keeps a man alive?
He feeds on others.
—Bertolt Brecht, *The Threepenny Opera*

ALL THE WAY BACK ON the train I could only think of one thing. I had to tell the others who had parents in Gurs that their mothers and fathers had been deported east. Or as the French put it, repatriated. There was no joke for this one. No song to make it easier. I returned in some kind of trance. I can hardly remember the journey. I arrived on the one o'clock train, which, as usual, was filled with refugees. I hurried through the village and up the trail to our house. Everyone was back in school after the summer break, so I had to wait until they returned. I washed in the stream, stripped bare since no one was there, and found some clean clothes. Then I sat at the kitchen table and waited.

The group burst through the door, laughing and talking. Rudi wasn't there, of course, he'd be doing his other work. They were thrilled to see me. I got hugs and kisses from everyone and was peppered with questions. Finally I put my hands up and said, "Stop! Stop! I have something to tell you. I saw most of your parents. They were—all right, but . . ." I paused trying to work up the courage to say the words. I took a deep breath. "They've all been deported back east."

There was dead silence.

"All?" said Klara in a whisper.

"All," I said.

One by one they moved away, some went to their rooms, most went out into the woods, so they could cry alone.

Later that day, just after dinner, which no one could eat despite Paul's prodding, Rudi showed up.

"Legs, you have to go see Pastor Trocmé."

"I do?"

"Yes. He's expecting you. He wants a report on what you saw down there."

"Rudi, I have to tell you something."

"I know," he said brusquely, "Klara told me. Go see the pastor."

It had never occurred to me to go to see Pastor Trocmé— I had other worries on my mind. But I understood immediately that he would want to hear about the deportations.

"Meet me at the farm, afterward," Rudi said. "There are a lot of deliveries tonight."

I had one more thing to do before I could talk to Pastor Trocmé. I sat at the kitchen table and wrote Ilse and Max. Ilse had only written me once in Le Chambon. She was having a hard time in England. Max wrote more often, short letters, just to let me know that he was fine. What words could I use to make it hurt less? I gritted my teeth and made myself do it.

When I got to the presbytery I told the Trocmés what I

had seen, and I asked them to mail the letters to my family.

Then I hurried to meet Rudi. He gave me two sets of false IDs, one for an adult, one for a child, and told me where they were staying—on a farm not too far from the village. The night was cool, so I ran most of the way to keep warm. When I got there, an old farmer let me in and pointed to the kitchen table where a woman in her late twenties sat with her daughter, who looked around eight or nine years old. I handed them their papers and the woman burst into tears.

"Don't cry, Maman," the little girl said, "now we are safe."

"Are you French?" the woman asked, clutching both my hands in hers.

"No, Madame," I said—although I spoke with no accent by then— "I'm from Mannheim."

"Don't let them catch you! Don't let them catch you," she wailed.

"Madame, please," I said, "don't trouble yourself. They won't catch me." I looked beseechingly at the farmer who shrugged, as if to say, I don't know what to do with her.

"Where have you come from?" I asked, thinking that maybe if I could get her talking I could calm her down. I couldn't help but think of Oma on the train, and how easy it is to go crazy.

"You know they asked all Jews in Paris to register. Why did we do it? We all did! We didn't have to. Our last name is Langlois, we could easily have passed for French—my parents came here from Poland years ago, my children were born here, are nationalized French. But we were proud. We didn't want to deny being Jews. And we were sure the

French would protect us. Hadn't they promised us?"

"Yes," I said, "of course they did."

"On Thursday, suddenly I was woken by a terrible scream. I ran to the window! Oh! What I saw!" And she began to weep uncontrollably.

Her daughter, a beautiful child with pale white skin, big hazel eyes, and long dark hair, spoke for her mother.

"I saw it, too," she said solemnly. "Mrs. Horowitz threw both of her children out the window. Then herself. They're all dead," she assured me.

I tried not to show the shock I felt.

"But why?"

"The police had come for us, don't you see," her mother said. "The police had come. The roundup. We'd heard rumors. But I was too stupid, we should've fled, we should've run."

"But we did, Maman," her daughter reassured her.

"Too late," her mother said. "But I tried. I grabbed Suzette and my husband grabbed Jean and we ran. The police chased us. French police. They could have looked the other way!"

"And when they caught us," Suzette continued, "we had to go to my school and wait in the auditorium with the other Jews. And then we were put on buses."

"They took us to the Vélodrome d'Hiver, the big sports arena on rue Nelaton," the mother continued. "There were thousands—one guard told me eight thousand in that place. We were there five days! They'd turned off the water, so there was nothing to drink and no water in the bathrooms. There was no food until the Red Cross and the Quakers tried to help. No beds, only the arena benches. There were sick people there. Mothers gave birth. They weren't taken to the hospital, they were left to do it in public, in the filth. People got dysentery from what little food there was. Most of the bathrooms were closed because they thought people might escape through the windows. The few toilets that were available got plugged up right away. You had to do your business right in the open—what choice did you have? The smell, the stench."

She wept, head in her hands.

"They treated you worse than animals," I said.

"That's true. In fact, animals were allowed to stay behind but not children. People tried to kill themselves, people went mad, I saw a mother try to cut her daughter's wrists with a broken bottle." She took a deep breath. "But I wouldn't let them get Suzette. Would I, Suzette?"

"No, Maman, you wouldn't," Suzette answered proudly.

"I couldn't find my husband and Jean," the mother continued. "But I knew we had to try to get out. You see, children under sixteen weren't supposed to be taken, but they could only be left behind if there was a grandparent older than sixty-five in the home. Both my parents are dead," she said, "so they made us take Jean and Suzette. Our neighbors would have cared for them, but the police refused to allow it. So I told Suzette to just walk out! That's right! Walk out and say she'd been visiting me!"

Suzette looked at me. "I did. I told the guard I'd been visiting and he let me out. And then Maman tried to get out, but they kept stopping her."

"But I found one guard who looked the other way," the woman said. "One guard. And we ran. We'd heard about Jews coming to the Haute-Loire, so we came here. That was almost six weeks ago. We've been hiding with friends along the way."

"You were very brave," I said. "And resourceful."

Suzette sat on her mother's lap and hugged her. "She's a good mommy."

"Yes," I said, "she is."

"You must be ready for the worst," her mother said. "The French are in it with the Nazis now."

"But not here," I reminded her.

"No," she said, "not here."

"So you'll be all right now. When do you leave?"

"Tomorrow, first thing, now that we have our papers."

I leaned over and kissed her on both cheeks. "I wish you every luck," I said.

She looked at me then, clearly, for the first time. She drew in a deep breath. "Thank you, my dear. I feel better now."

"Of course you do," I said. "And *you're* very brave too," I said to Suzette. "You'll take good care of your mother, I know."

She nodded, like she was all grown up, which in a way, she was.

Just a week later Le Chambon got its first visit from some of the big officials in the Vichy government, including the minister of youth, Georges Lamirand, and Prefect Bach, the prefect in charge of this entire area. The Vichy government had tried to copy a lot of Hitler's policies on youth, from saluting the flag in schools (which no one in the Cévenole School would do) to setting up youth camps based on the Hitler Youth. It was disgusting, I thought, pathetically mimicking the very worst of the Nazis. My friends were furious that he was coming. Of course, we were quite a mix of students at the Cévenole School; boys who had refused to attend these youth camps; young men who had fled here to escape forced labor; French children who attended the school; and the Jewish refugees. But we *all* agreed that the roundup of the Jews in Paris was a disgrace. So the older theological students put together a letter to give to the minister. We weren't there but Robert, one of the students, told us all about it later that night.

"At the YMCA camp luncheon, when the officials first arrived, one of the Girl Scouts serving spilled hot soup down Minister Lamirand's back." Robert laughed. "After lunch they marched through the village, but everyone in town ignored them so the streets were empty. They gave their speeches when they arrived at the sports field. Monsieur Poiter cited St. Paul, and kept stressing the idea, 'You should love your neighbor as yourself.' I'm sure that was lost on Lamirand completely. Then I walked right up to Lamirand and read him the letter:

'Mr. Minister,

'We have learned of the frightening scenes that took place three weeks ago in Paris, where the French police, on orders of the occupying power, arrested in their homes all the Jewish families in Paris to hold *them in the Vel d'Hiv. The fathers were torn from their families and sent to Germany. The children torn from their mothers, who underwent the same fate as their husbands. Knowing by experience that the decrees of the occupying power are, with brief delay, imposed on Unoccupied France, where they are presented as spontaneous decisions of the head of the French government, we are afraid that the measures of deportation of the Jews will soon be applied in the Southern Zone.*

'We feel obliged to tell you that there are among us a certain number of Jews. But, we make no distinction between Jews and non-Jews. It is contrary to the gospel teaching.

'If our comrades, whose only fault is to be born in another religion, received the order to let themselves be deported, or even examined, they would disobey the orders received, and we would try to hide them as best we could.'

"Minister Lamirand replied, in this really cold voice, 'This isn't my business. It is the prefect's affair.'

"The prefect was furious. He turned to Pastor Trocmé. 'The government knows what it is doing. It has ordered the regrouping of all European Jews in order to send them to Poland. In a few days my people will come to round up the Jews living in Le Chambon.'

"Pastor Trocmé replied, 'We do not know what a Jew is. We only know men.'

"Prefect Bach glared at Pastor Trocmé. 'If you are not prudent, it is you whom I shall be obliged to have arrested.'"

The group sitting around Robert said nothing. We were all frightened. After all, Pastor Trocmé was like the rock of Le Chambon. I didn't see him much, but somehow he seemed to have a hand in everything. What would happen if he was taken away? I worried for him, but I worried for us too. Would we still be safe? And after the deportations in Paris, and Gurs, how much longer would they leave us here?

TEN

Some men are born great, some achieve greatness,
and some have greatness thrust upon them.
—Shakespeare, *Twelfth Night*

AS I FEARED, THE FRENCH gendarmes did appear one day, to arrest us. That's why Klara and I are now on the run.

It happened like this.

Paul was suddenly called away—his father had taken ill and Paul had to go see him. He put me in charge of the house.

That night I didn't go to help Rudi, but when he came home he had troubling news. Madame Philip, who was one of the resistance leaders in Le Chambon, had heard from her contact in St. Étienne that a raid might be forthcoming. I decided that we couldn't stay alone in the farmhouse—I made everyone get dressed, and we tramped down the path to the Red Cross house at the bottom of the hill. Denis was in charge there—he wasn't much older than Rudi, but I hoped that they might skip this house. Our house had more Jews registered, and they were sure to go there first. We all slept on the floor, Denis was happy to have us.

It was the middle of the night when a loud knocking woke us all. You could hear a pin drop as Denis made his way to the door. There stood the gendarmes, and they demanded that any Jews in the house go with them. Denis was incredible. He simply refused.

"Every child in this house is under Swiss protection," he declared. "You have no jurisdiction here. Go away. Do you want to create an international incident? If you know what's good for you, you'll leave at once."

Well, they didn't leave at once. They argued, but Denis, a boy nearly half their age, went on and on with such conviction that finally they agreed to go to the authorities in Le Puy and check the story.

"But," I heard one of them warn, "you had better have every single one here when we get back."

And amazingly they all left! Why they didn't leave anyone behind to guard us I'll never know. Perhaps the feelings of the village people were catching, and they found it hard to put their hearts into rounding us up when no one would help them.

"Everyone must go into the woods," Denis ordered as soon as they left. "Go and hide. Don't worry. We'll come and find you and get you to safe places. Go! Go!"

We scrambled out of the house, Klara holding Rudi's hand, me right beside them. Everyone split up. The three of us hurried quite deep into the woods and finally settled down in a spot that seemed well protected.

"That was a close call," Rudi said. "Now listen, you two are going to be all right here. I have to go."

"Go where?" exclaimed Klara. "You can't go."

"I have to get to Madame Philip," Rudi said. "Everyone is going to need false papers now—like you two, for instance. I've got *lots* of work to do."

Klara clutched at his arms. "Rudi, you can't go!"

Slowly he pried her hands off him and put them in mine.

"You'll look after her, legs, won't you?"

"Of course I will!" I said, trying to sound indignant. Trying not to let him hear how flattered I was that he thought I was more mature and capable than his own sister. "If you stop calling me 'legs.'"

"I could do that," he agreed. "Anni is also nice."

"Not Anni. Anna!"

"Sorry, Anni is the best I can do, legs," he said. "I mean . . . Anni." He got up. "Don't worry. I'll find you both." And he was gone.

"Maybe we should just give ourselves up," Klara said. "This is too nerve-racking."

"And what would happen then? Would the French take care of us or hand us right over to the Nazis?"

"You're right," Klara said, "I know. But sometimes I wonder if it's worth it."

"What do you mean?" I asked. Although I thought I knew, I hoped I was wrong.

"Everything. Living. Maybe it isn't worth it. Even if we live. What can we look forward to? Having children. Maybe seeing them murdered. Or they can watch their parents being murdered. What's the point?"

It was horrible, but I had no answer. What if she was right? What if the world was so horrible, we'd be better off dead? Maybe we should just leave it to Hitler and his Nazis. Let evil take over completely. Why not? It seemed like it had anyway.

So I didn't answer. I just held on to her hand, and we both leaned against a tree. Finally, I suppose we both fell asleep.

When the sun woke us we were starving, but, of course, there was no food. We picked berries all day, and talked. Finally, near dark we heard a whistle.

Was it a good whistle or a bad whistle? We had no way of knowing. Was it someone from the village or one of the French gendarmes?

"We have to run," Klara hissed.

"Not yet," I whispered back. "What if it's someone sent to help us?"

"How will we know?"

"You wait here. I'll circle around and see if I can catch a glimpse of whoever it is."

Klara huddled down behind a bush. I crept slowly in a circle toward the sound of the whistle. The air smelled sweet with pine needles and flowers. Twigs cracked under my feet. I cursed, silently. And then I saw him. It was Maurice. Relieved, I ran over to him, then led him to where Klara was hiding.

We all knew Maurice. He was a Boy Scout leader.

"Come on," Maurice said to us, "we've found a safe place for both of you." And he led us to the Debard farmhouse. Just after we got there I said to Klara, "Remember what you said in the woods?"

"Yes."

"When you see how everyone in this whole area is working to save us, even knowing what could happen to them if they are caught, do you still feel the same way?"

She paused for a moment, then her eyes met mine.

"How could I?" she said.

I smiled at her. "You couldn't."

Monsieur Chave walks into the house just as Klara and I are finishing breakfast.

"Look who's here," he says, and Guy comes running in.

"Guy!" I exclaim. "Are you all right? Is your family all right?"

"Yes," he nods. "I came here looking for you. I thought maybe you'd think of coming to Grand-père's house."

"Are you Guy's grandfather?" I asked Monsieur Chave, quite surprised.

"Paulette is our daughter." Madame Chave smiles. "That's why the farms are so close. She and her husband took over part of our land when they married." She looks at Guy. "No trouble?"

"No," Guy grins. "Maman told the gendarmes she didn't know the girls were hiding there, and she was so nice to them, giving them coffee after they fell in the manure pit, and they were so upset they just wanted to get away and get changed!"

Madame Chave chuckles. "They fell in your manure pit?"

I laugh out loud, remembering.

"And one of them had on a brand-new uniform!" Guy adds. He turns to us. "They weren't shooting at you, you know. The gun went off when one of them fell. They were really silly. The only smart one was their dog. He was the one that sniffed you out. But our dogs took care of him, don't worry!"

"Have you heard anything else, Guy?" I asked. "Has anyone been caught?"

"Early this morning Maman sent me to town to see what I could find out. We were worried maybe you'd been captured. When I got there I saw three empty buses come into the marketplace. And the chief of police was there."

Madame Chave interjects. "The chief of the entire Haute-Loire region. How honored we must feel!"

"And they made Pastor Trocmé come to the town hall. I hid in the corridor and listened."

I have to hide a smile. A little resistance fighter in the making.

"The chief scolded Pastor Trocmé," Guy says obviously shocked by this. "He was rude!"

"But what did he say, dear?" Madame Chave asks.

"A lot of big words. And that he knew that Pastor Trocmé was hiding Jews. And that he wanted a list of the Jews and where they live."

"What did Pastor Trocmé say?" asks Klara.

"That he didn't know the people's names and that even if he had a list he wouldn't give it to the chief because these people had come here for help and . . . and . . ."

"What?" we all say.

"I'm trying to remember," Guy says, frowning. "Something about being a shepherd. Not the police chief. Pastor Trocmé said that he was our shepherd! And a shepherd doesn't, well he used a big word, but he doesn't give away his sheep." Guy looks at us. "Of course he doesn't!

We all know that. What a terrible shepherd that would be."

I laugh aloud. So does Klara.

"They haven't caught *one* person yet," Guy says triumphantly. "Not one!"

ELEVEN

Many waters cannot quench love,
Neither can the floods drown it.
        —*Song of Solomon*

I SMILE FOR THE CAMERA. I am getting my picture taken for my false identification papers. "All right, girls," Rudi says, "I'll have your papers in a few days. In the meantime, we have a contact who will warn us if any more raids are coming, so, until then, you can go back to school, and we can all go back to the Red Cross houses to live."

I roll my eyes. School. Although, I suppose, it won't be that bad. Madame Chave and her husband were wonderful to Klara and me while the buses sat in the village square for over a week and the gendarmes looked for Jews. But they had very few books as they are from a strict fundamental Christian background. So I read the Bible. Actually, it was pretty interesting—and they gave me the Old Testament so I wouldn't feel uncomfortable. They called Klara and me God's children. It is in their belief that the Jewish people are special to God, and they felt it was a privilege to help us.

They are very poor and had so little extra food to share that one night they sent Klara and me out to capture and kill frogs. Madame Chave fried them and that night we had frogs' legs for dinner. But I'll eat anything. At Gurs we ate cow udders, so frogs don't seem half as bad.

We had one other close call while we were there. The gendarmes came to search the Chave farm. They had nowhere to hide us, so Madame Chave put us in the wardrobe, our feet in Monsieur Chave's big shoes. I was terrified. So was Klara. It felt like we were there for hours. We heard Madame Chave say, "Jews? I don't even know what one looks like!" Fortunately I was too scared to laugh.

Finally, the gendarmes gave up.

Rudi is smiling to himself.

"What's so funny?" I ask him.

"Oh. I was just thinking about what some of the village boys painted on the main street a few days before the gendarmes left."

I smile too. " 'One cannot catch them, those Jewish boys.' Actually," I say, tossing my hair, "I'm quite insulted. One couldn't catch those Jewish girls either!"

"Not with legs like that," Rudi grins.

"Hey! I thought we had a deal. No more with the legs!"

"Did we? Funny, I don't seem to recall."

"Klara! Make him stop," I say.

"Make Rudi stop?" Klara grimaces. "I've never figured out how."

"So the gendarmes just left?" I ask Rudi.

"They just gave up and left," Rudi confirms. "But you know they did catch someone—except I've heard that since he has only two Jewish grandparents he'll soon be released. He sat all alone on the bus, and everyone from the village brought him treats. The gendarmes must really have felt like idiots.

"Oh, and something else happened that was quite funny. You know Marc, he was in my class at Cévenole School?"

"Yes," we both say.

"Well, he was sitting under a tree reading a book. And this gendarme stops quite a bit away and tries to get his attention. He's calling to him, you know, 'Pssst, pssst.' Finally Marc looks up from his book and then the gendarme starts to make funny gestures. Marc had no idea what he was doing. Finally, the gendarme goes right up to Marc and says, 'Go away, I haven't seen you.' So Marc is still completely in the dark and asks the gendarme what on earth he's talking about. The gendarme explains that since he's looking for Jews, if Marc doesn't beat it fast, the gendarme will be *forced* to arrest him. Marc laughs and says, 'But I'm not Jewish!' 'Oh you aren't one of them? So much the better. I don't like the job they have given us.'"

Klara giggles. "I can just see Marc," she says. "He must have thought the guard was mad!"

"Enough visiting," Rudi declares. "I'd better get to work on this. I'll see you two later."

That night, when I go to help Rudi with his deliveries, he tells me that there have been lots of new people arriving over the last few days, almost all Jewish.

"Really? Where are they?" I ask. "I haven't noticed."

"As soon as they get here, they are taken in," he explains. "Almost every farm in the area is hiding someone. A lot of them are coming in through a Jewish resistance group called Service André. And then CIMADE and many of the other groups are helping to get some of them to Switzerland."

I have a very busy night and get back exhausted. I have just gotten ready for bed when Rudi appears and motions me to follow him onto the balcony. I grab a sweater and put it over my nightgown, as the air is getting cold now at night.

"You and Klara leave tomorrow for Switzerland," Rudi says. "I've got it all arranged."

For a moment I am too shocked to respond.

"Just like that?"

"No, not just like that. It took quite a bit of organizing."

"Who asked you?"

"Don't you want to go?"

"I don't know."

"What do you mean, you don't know? Are you crazy?"

"No, I'm not! Maybe I want to stay here."

"Well," says Rudi, beginning to look very angry, "you'd better explain why."

"Maybe I want to help this Service André," I say quietly. "Maybe I want to join the resistance."

"Hah!"

He is laughing at me!

"You don't think I could fight? I know the resistance has a network around here. I know a lot of them live right here in town. And I know that they train out in the woods. Well," I say defiantly, "they can train me."

"And do you think Klara can fight too?"

"No," I admit, "she couldn't."

"And how many raids do you think it'll take before Klara becomes a nervous wreck? Even if she isn't caught, how long do you think she'll be able to stand constantly running and hiding? Because this first raid was just the beginning, you know *that* don't you?"

"But Rudi, the trip to Switzerland will be nerve-racking too!"

"I know," he says, pacing. "But I have to do what I think is best. It's dangerous, but if you make it, you'll be safe." He pauses. "Both of you."

"Well," I say, "I'm glad to see that you care just a little about me as well. . . ."

I stop, because suddenly he is standing right in front of me, and the moon hits his face so I can see his eyes, and they are so intense, he is staring at me. . . .

"Rudi?"

Slowly he tilts his head and I feel paralyzed, or hypnotized or something, because I can't move, and then he kisses me. His lips just touch mine, so softly, I had no idea he was capable of such gentleness. Then he looks me in the eye again, both hands on my shoulders.

"Well, well, well." It is Klara.

Rudi and I leap apart. Rudi turns away, but I can see that he is blushing because even his neck has turned red, almost the color of his hair.

"What's going on?" she asks.

"Rudi is sending us to Switzerland tomorrow," I say, although I find that my voice is shaking. "Whether we want to go or not." I'm sure that's not what she meant when she asked what was going on, but my answer must at least make her forget what she just saw.

"I'm ready to go," Klara says.

This night is full of surprises. "You are?"

"Yes," she says, "I am. It's only going to be more raids, more hiding. If we can go, then I think we should."

"Not me, Klara," Rudi says. "I can't. I have too much work to do here."

"Then I won't go either," Klara states.

"But legs here won't go without you, Klara," Rudi says. "So you *have* to go."

I glare at Rudi. He knows very well it's the other way around. He looks at me, pleading. I have to think fast. He's probably right. Klara needs me to take her. And if I can get her there safely, then maybe I can slip back here to help. Who knows?

"He's right, Klara." I sigh. "I won't go if you won't. It's all arranged. I think we'd better just do it."

Rudi goes over to Klara and gives her a hug. "We're all that's left of the family," he says. "So you be sure to get there safely."

She hugs him back.

He looks at me. "Thanks, legs."

For a moment our eyes meet, then he's gone.

"Did he kiss you?" Klara asks.

"You saw."

"I'm not surprised."

"You're *not*?"

"Oh, no. I've known he's been nuts over you for ages now."

"He has a funny way of showing it."

She smiles. "He does, doesn't he? Like a little boy throwing sticks at you to get your attention because he likes you."

I smile. "You're right."

"Come on," she says. "We'd better pack our knapsacks and say good-bye to the others."

"I'm not going to be able to sleep a wink tonight," I say to her as we go into the house.

"Me either," she replies.

But it's not because we're leaving. Well, it is of course. But it's also that kiss. I keep feeling Rudi's lips on mine and I can't get it out of my mind because I liked it. I really liked it. Why did he have to wait until just before I leave to do it? Honestly, he's maddening, really maddening. But what eyes!

TWELVE

I have been a stranger in a strange land.
—*Exodus*

THE GOOD-BYES ARE SAID in a blur of hugs and kisses and good wishes. Rudi brusquely gives me a peck on the cheek, hugs Klara, then leaves. It turns out that Peter is coming with us. I'm a bit worried about him, he's such a hothead. But he isn't stupid and if we need to fight he'll be ready.

Rudi has explained our route to us so we start off right after breakfast. We walk to the nearby village of Tence and find the house of the pastor there, where we have to stay all day. We're too well known in Le Chambon and Rudi didn't want the gendarmes to see us leaving. The next morning we catch the train for Lyon.

The station at Lyon is crowded, but we manage to get tickets to Annecy, quite near the Swiss border. The train doesn't leave for hours so we each sit in a different corner, trying to look invisible. When we get on the train there are gendarmes everywhere. I decide to go stand right beside them to show that I have nothing to hide. Klara sits, her nose in a magazine, except the magazine shakes because her hands are trembling. Finally we reach Annecy and we are met by another pastor, Pastor Muril. We sleep that night in his home, on the floor, and just before dawn we set off on foot, to climb the mountain separating us from Switzerland, the Cheval Blanc, Pastor Muril leading us.

It is pouring rain. We are all wearing regular shoes. We had to give up our wooden clogs. They might have drawn attention to us on the train, as they are typically worn by people in small mountain villages. My shoes are too tight. Klara's are too loose so she's stuffed little pieces of flannel in them. Peter's are full of holes. Pastor Muril has shoes with cleats. I look at them enviously.

For the last two days Klara, Peter, and I have barely spoken to each other. We've been scared, I suppose, and feeling lonely and anxious. Are we doing the right thing? Would we have been better off staying put? Will we make it?

We are all wearing coats and Klara and I both have kerchiefs on our head, but it is raining so hard that soon even my thick hair is soaked through. We slog up the mountain path, yellow leaves around our feet. We climb all day, only stopping to catch our breath. Finally, as night falls, Pastor Muril leads us to a small woodshed. We are thankful to be out of the rain and wind.

Pastor Muril is a round, small man, with beady eyes. But when he smiles, he looks like a little child, happy without a concern in the world. "Look!" He grins, and he brings cold boiled potatoes out of his rucksack as if they are gold. As far as I'm concerned, they *are* gold. We eat them, then curl up on the floor, and, somehow, fall asleep.

As soon as the sun rises over the mountain we are on our way again. Within an hour we find ourselves slogging through snow. I begin to feel quite lightheaded.

"We're getting up to around nine thousand feet above sea level here." Pastor Muril grins. "Makes you feel light as an angel."

"I could use an angel right about now," I pant, "to fly me the rest of the way."

"If angels existed," scoffs Peter, "do you think we'd be here in the first place? Sorry, Pastor, but it's pretty hard to believe in that sort of thing, you'd have to agree."

"But I don't," says Pastor Muril, puffing heavily. "I believe in angels. I think they're as real as we are. And I'm sure they are, even now, helping where they can. And crying for those they can't help."

"Excuse me, Pastor, but that just sounds pathetic to me," says Peter. "I mean, if God wanted to help, He'd help. Nothing could stop Him."

"Nothing but Himself. The laws of our universe are set. He can't suddenly change them because we humans have chosen Satan over Him."

"I don't believe in Satan," Peter declares.

"No," says the pastor, "you wouldn't. It isn't part of the Jewish belief."

"And do you know why?" asks Peter.

"Why?" asks the pastor, which I think is very nice of him because he must know so he's just being kind to Peter, letting him talk.

"Because it's dangerous to split good and evil like that, as if evil is something outside ourselves. Until we all realize we're capable of evil, we'll all continue to *do* evil. Each of us has a devil inside us."

"Not me!" I say, trying to lighten the mood. "Certainly not Klara. She's perfect."

Peter gazes at Klara for a moment. "Yes. Maybe Klara," he says.

"Well!" I say indignantly. "Thanks a lot!"

Just then Klara drops to her knees, then sort of falls over.

"Klara!" Peter exclaims. "What is it?"

"It's the lack of oxygen," says the pastor.

"Wait a minute," I say, rummaging in my knapsack. I pull out a cube of sugar and hurry over to Klara with it.

"Klara! Klara! Wake up." She opens her eyes.

"Open your mouth." She does. I pop in the sugar cube.

She eats it, and I give her another. After a few minutes she seems to revive. I can't do anything about the thin air, but at least the sugar can give her some extra energy. Peter is hovering over her like a mother bear.

"Klara? Are you all right?"

"Yes, Peter, I'm fine. I just got dizzy all of a sudden. I'll be fine. But my feet feel almost numb."

"Let me look," Peter says. Gently he takes off her shoes and her socks. "Your toes are almost white!" He takes some snow and rubs her feet with the snow until they turn red. Then he massages them until they are closer to a regular color. I follow his example and rub my own feet, and then he rubs his, as well. I suppose we're all in danger of losing our toes altogether, to frostbite.

Finally we begin again, but things only get worse. We have to climb up rocky ledges and small vertical paths. I am cursing Rudi. This *certainly* is worse than hiding in a farmhouse in Le Chambon. Suddenly Klara gets panicky and won't move. She turns to me.

"I can't do that," she says. She is pointing to a thin ledge we have to maneuver across. Below is a sheer drop into nothing.

"Yes, you can," I say. "Look, Peter will go first, then you, and I'll be right behind you. We won't let anything happen to you."

"I can't!" she says.

"Klara. We can't go back down this way," I say. "We have no choice. Pastor Muril has done this many times before. He knows what he's doing. Right, Pastor?" I say.

"Of course," says the pastor.

Peter takes Klara's hand. "Come," he says. "I'll go first. You follow. Just keep your eyes on me."

I think I see Klara blush a bit. Why would she like him? She's so sweet and he's all angles and hard edges.

"All right," she agrees. First Pastor Muril goes, taking little steps, one by one, his back against the rock, until he's on the tiny path on the other side. Then Peter, with Klara right behind him, me right behind Klara. We are all coaching Klara.

"One more step. You can do it. Come on, Klara. Keep going."

I keep my hands against the rough rock, leaning back into the mountain. She is taking little baby steps. But, finally, she's across.

And I am—I am hanging in the air. For a moment I am so stunned I can't figure out what's happened. Then I hear Klara scream. And I realize that I must have slipped. I'm hanging over nothing.

"Stay there, stay there," Peter says, "I'm coming. Your knapsack has caught on a rock and is holding you."

Stay here? Where should I go? Peter edges back onto the ledge. Then he calls, "I've got a hold of your knapsack. See if you can pull yourself up."

Slowly I turn myself around, my heart pounding, my breath coming in short gasps. I reach up and feel for the ledge. It's there. I put one hand on it, then the other.

"I'll pull your knapsack; you pull yourself," Peter says. "Ready?"

"Ready."

"One, two. *Three!*"

I grab the ledge, dig my fingers in, and pull with all my strength. I get one knee up, then the other. Finally I am back on the ledge, and Peter and I shuffle across. I fall into Klara's arms.

"Oh, my God," she says. "Oh, my God!"

"I'm all right," I pant, but I'm shaking.

Peter goes into my knapsack and comes out with the sugar.

"Take it," he says.

"No, Klara will need it."

"Take it!" Klara orders.

I put the cube in my mouth, and suck on it. A few minutes go by and I stop shaking. As we get up to continue on, Pastor Muril says to Peter, "Perhaps there was an angel here with you right now. To me, that was a miracle."

Peter shakes his head. "If the angel had been doing his job Anna wouldn't have fallen in the first place."

We reach a small stone hut and we are able to rest for a

while. But not too long. We continue on and finally start to descend, which for a while is easier. But soon the terrain flattens into snow and ice and grass all mixed together. It becomes incredibly slippery. Since Pastor Muril is the only one with decent shoes he goes first, and we slip and slide behind him. At one point, we are faced with a long ledge of ice, and Pastor Muril decides that he must help us down one by one. First he takes Klara. He comes back for me, and when we are almost at the bottom Klara yells, "Peter, wait for help!" I glance up to see Peter starting down on his own.

"I'll be fine," he calls back, but just then he slips and he begins to slide, and soon he's on his back, sliding feet first.

"There's a sheer drop over that edge," Pastor Muril exclaims. He lets go of me.

By now Peter is barreling down, going so fast I don't see how he can be stopped. Klara is standing, hand over her mouth, watching in horror. As soon as the pastor lets go of me he moves quickly, especially for someone so stout, until he is right in front of Peter's downward slide. He throws his own body down directly in front of Peter. Peter crashes into the pastor with a horrible thump, pushing the pastor right to the edge where they both finally come to a stop.

I take a deep breath and shake my head in relief. Klara slips and slides over to them and begins to swat Peter.

"You idiot! Couldn't you have waited? Do you always have to do everything by yourself? You can't take a little help?"

Peter looks up, at first bewildered by the ferocity of her attack, but it doesn't take him long to realize that she wouldn't be hitting him if she didn't care for him. He beams at her like a little child getting Hanukkah gelt. Pastor Muril sees him beaming and that makes him beam. Klara glares at Peter.

"And you can wipe that smile off your face."

He does so immediately, replacing it by a look of such meekness that I think Klara should be ashamed of driving him into this state. But she doesn't seem ashamed at all. Now *she's* beaming.

Finally we get going again, and it's not long before Pastor Muril says, "This is it. The border. I can't cross with you. You have to continue down this glacier. Near the bottom you'll reach a waterfall and on the other side of that is a path."

We thank him profusely and we start off on our own.

THIRTEEN

Man is born unto trouble, as the sparks fly upward.
—Job

IT IS EVENING, the sun is setting fast, and we are lost in the mountains. Klara is trying not to cry. Peter is holding her hand, making soothing noises, as I desperately try to find a way out. We found the waterfall with no problem, but here we are, the mountain on our left, the waterfall on our right, and nowhere to go. I can't see any path and I can't see any way for us to get across the base of the waterfall without drowning. I've already slipped on the rocks once and needed Peter to pull me out of the swirling water. I sit on a rock, trying not to panic. We could die out here! We can't go back, we can't go forward; it's getting very cold and we have no food left. I stare into the water. Is that something glinting? I look closer. It is. I check the rocks around me and find a place where I can put one foot in the water and hang on to a rock with one arm. I lean into the water. It looks like something silver.

"Peter!" I call. "Come here."

He hurries over. "What is it?"

"Hang on to that branch," I order, "and give me your other arm. I want to see something."

Peter anchors himself, one arm on a tree branch, and gives me the other. I place my foot farther in the water, trying to see what is glinting there. I think it's a sardine can, which means people must have been here. As I look up I notice that on the other side, just downstream from where I'm leaning, there is a small opening in the rocks and water.

"I think I see a way out!"

The water is pounding and swirling, so we make a small chain. Peter anchors, holding on to the same tree branch, then Klara, then me. I find, as I wade across, that the water isn't as strong or as deep as it looks. In a minute I'm across, and I wave to them to follow. Klara slips at one point, but Peter is right behind her and catches her. Once on the other side we maneuver between rocks and some water until, suddenly, a path opens up, winding down the mountain.

I let out a whoop, Klara and Peter join in. Whatever happens, at least we won't be trapped on the mountain. Just before it gets completely dark we find that the path leads us right to a Swiss construction crew, just finishing work for the day on a road that intersects our path. We approach them, and they are very friendly and I begin to feel that maybe, just maybe, we've made it! Two Swiss policemen approach us, and we explain that we are Jewish refugees from France.

One of them shakes his head and says, "I'm sorry. You'll have to go back."

"What?" Peter says, his voice threatening.

When the policeman hears Peter's tone his voice becomes harsh. "You heard me. The Swiss government is *not* allowing any Jewish refugees in right now. Only people with legitimate visas. You'll have to go back to France."

"If we go back, we'll be sent east. We'll be killed."

"It's nothing to do with us. That's the law right now."

"Look," says the other, "we'll let you cross where there aren't any French guards so you won't be arrested. And you can get something to eat first."

"Oh, thank you," says Peter, his voice dripping with sarcasm. "Thank you so much."

I'm too disappointed to speak. We follow the policemen into a small mountain inn, where we use some of the money we have to buy food. "We may as well eat," Peter says bitterly. So we have some soup and a stew with real meat in it.

When we finish eating, and have used the washrooms, the guards take us by truck to Vallorcine. They send us over the border, and my heart sinks as I see French gendarmes coming toward us.

Peter shakes his head. "Those bastards," he says, and I know he doesn't just mean those Swiss police. He also means the Swiss government, the Swiss people. Why do they hate us so much they won't even let us take refuge in their country?

"Remember," says Klara, "it's the Swiss that are taking care of us in Le Chambon."

"The Swiss Red Cross," I say. "I agree with Peter. It's no reflection on their government or their policies, that the Red Cross wants to help. All the relief organizations are trying to help while their governments are trying to kill us."

The gendarmes handcuff us and put us on a truck. We are driven to La Voulte-sur-Rhône and then just left in the truck for the rest of the night. Handcuffed. I can't imagine where they are about to take us. I don't even want to think about it.

In the morning we continue our drive until we stop just outside a huge complex of barracks, which looks frighteningly similar to Gurs.

"Where are we?" I shout to our driver.

"A camp called Rivesaltes," he replies.

And before we know it we are in a barracks, with both men and women in it, surrounded by people who look thin, exhausted, malnourished and who have all sorts of questions for us. All I can think is that we're in a place just like Gurs, where we will no doubt end up like our parents. Klara is clinging to me, weeping quietly. I tell Peter to take her over into a corner, and I try to answer all the questions I am asked.

We are interrupted by an announcement, obviously by one of the camp leaders.

"Everyone is to pack," he says. "The deportations start today."

I look at Klara and Peter in a panic. I run over to the man who's just made the announcement.

"Is the CIMADE here in this camp?" I ask.

"Yes."

"Where?"

He points out their barracks to me. I hurry over there only to find it full of people pleading with the CIMADE workers to somehow get them off the deportation lists. I wait my turn. When I introduce myself, the young woman listens intently as I tell my story.

"You're Madame Lévy's children, aren't you?" she asks, referring to Madame Lévy from OSE who helped us flee Gurs.

I nod.

"I'll try," she says. "And I'll let them know where you are."

"You will?" I say, for the first time feeling some hope.

"I will."

I go back to tell Klara and Peter. Soon the names are called in the barracks. We hold our breath, but we aren't called. About half the people in the barracks leave. We find bunks. At dinner we are given some watery soup. No one can live on this. I don't know how we survived before. As night falls I am so miserable I feel like giving up. So I sing. I sing every song I can think of. Soon the barracks is full of people, and someone has gotten a violin, and someone else a flute, and we play music and sing into the early hours of the morning until I am so exhausted I can't think anymore, and then finally, I sleep.

In the morning I wake up to find Madame Philip from Le Chambon standing over my bunk. I really don't know her all that well, but I throw myself into her arms as if she is my best friend. Maybe, at this moment, she is.

"Don't worry," she says. "We're going to get you out of here, back to Le Chambon. We're going to try at any rate. I promise."

We all know that there is only so much they can do, but just to know that there is someone who cares for us and knows where we are makes us feel better. It turns out that Madame Philip was in the area on some kind of mission.

But a day passes. Then another day. And another. And another. And no one comes for us.

Men and women are allowed in the same barracks for some reason, so Klara and Peter begin to spend all their time together. As for me, I immediately find the culture barracks and I spend my afternoon practicing for concerts. But so many have already been deported, there are only a few of us left who can make music. Still, we do what we can.

I am leading a group of young people, singing old folk songs, when Peter bursts into the barracks. "The Germans have occupied the Free Zone," he declares. "The camp director is calling a meeting."

We all hurry to the camp center in time to hear the director say, "All students and all political prisoners are free to leave."

Peter, Klara, and I stare at each other. We can't believe it. It's an actual little miracle.

The CIMADE worker finds us, gives us money, and tells us to be ready to leave on the early morning train. She takes us to the station and by four thirty in the afternoon, we, along with many others, get off the train in Le Chambon.

I have never felt so glad to be anywhere. Rudi is standing on the station platform. When we get off the train he runs to Klara and gives her a hug. He shakes Peter's hand. And then he looks at me for a moment, as if uncertain what to do. In one swift move he lopes over to me, lifts me in the air, twirls me around, then kisses me. And I don't mean a soft little kiss. I mean a real kiss, holding me so tight I can hardly breathe. He lets me go finally. I stare at him. I feel like rubbing my eyes to get the stardust out. Where did the clown go? All I can see is this incredibly handsome redhead, with big broad shoulders and clear green eyes. And where are his freckles? They must have faded without me noticing. His skin is clear now, if very pale. He's gorgeous!

"Why are you shaking your head like that, legs?" he says. "You look like a puppy just out of a bath."

"My eyes are acting up," I say.

He looks concerned. "You're all right, aren't you?"

He's worried! I grin. "I'm fine," I say.

"Good," he says, "because this time I have a surefire way for you to get to Switzerland. I'll need a week or so to organize it."

"Rudi!" Klara and I say together.

"What?" he says innocently. "Come on. You can't stay in the old house now, not with these papers. You're still officially under arrest."

"Do you know *everything*?"

"Yes," he says. "Madame Philip and I have been keeping a close eye on you. Let's go."

We follow him through the village as he leads us to an outlying farm, where we can hide.

Fourteen

The wolf also shall dwell with the lamb,
and the leopard shall lie down with the kid;
and the calf and the young lion and the fatling together;
and a little child shall lead them.

—Isaiah

IT IS OUR FOURTH DAY hiding with Monsieur and Madame Russier, on an outlying farm. Actually, Rudi is also staying here now, because his work has become too dangerous to continue right under the noses of the Germans, who have also arrived in Le Chambon. They have taken over one of the hotels on the main street, the one right across from resistance headquarters, and they plan to use it as a place for their wounded to recuperate. Right now Rudi is hiding his fake papers in the beehives on the farm. They should be pretty safe there. Monsieur and Madame Russier have three young children, yet they offer their help as if there is no risk at all involved.

They are very religious and read from the Old Testament every night. I actually find much of it fascinating, some of it is even beautiful. They read from Job last night. He certainly suffered. Peter, of course, found a line that he just loved: "Curse God, and die." How can Klara like someone who is so pessimistic *all* the time. It's depressing. Personally, I like the lines: "But where shall wisdom be found? And where is the place of understanding?"

Rudi has time for none of it. He's quit school and is now working full time on his forgeries. And he's managed to make us exit visas from France as well as entrance visas to Switzerland so that we can go across the border legally. None of us has bothered to argue with him, despite how hard it was last time—because with the Germans in Le Chambon, it's obvious that we'd all be safer out of here. Although, I'm not sure that I won't try to get back once I have Klara and Peter safely across. Rudi and I had quite a little argument about that, late last night, after he returned from his deliveries.

"You aren't coming back," he said, after I told him, as if it was up to him.

"It's not up to you," I said.

"Yes, it is."

"Well, this is really getting us somewhere. Are we going to sit here all night saying yes it is, no it isn't, to each other?"

"Look," he said, trying very hard to sound reasonable, as if he were speaking to a naughty child. "You'll be safe. You'll be with Klara. She'll still need you."

"Yes," I agree, "I'll be safe. But Klara won't need me. She'll have Peter. The only reason I'm even going with them now is that Peter is such a hothead, and he's so unpre-dictable, and I don't trust him to think straight should he need to. So I'll get them both to safety. Then we'll see."

"We won't see. If you try to come back here, you'll just

be caught again. And this time you won't be so lucky."

"I won't do it unless I can figure out a way so that I won't get caught."

"Promise?"

I stare at him.

"Promise me?"

"My mother always said that to me."

He reaches out and touches my face with his hand.

"I'm sorry." He opens his arms and in a moment I am encircled in them, and I find that I am crying, sobbing, the first time I've cried for her and Aunt Mina. I miss them so much. *Did they suffer,* I wonder, *when they died? Did they suffer a lot?* They had never hurt a soul in the world, they didn't deserve to die like that, at the hands of monsters.

I can't bear to think of it. In fact, I've tried so hard *not* to think of it. I don't even like to think about Max and Ilse. It makes me too sad. Too lonely.

When I had calmed down a little I looked up at Rudi and said, "Rudi, I may *have* to come back and fight. Even if it puts me in danger. The same way you have to. Someone has to stop them. And I have a sister, and a brother, still alive. With your family, it's just you and Klara. And you'll *never* be sensible. So I'll help Klara. Then we'll see."

We stayed like that for a long time, holding each other tight.

"Ready?" Rudi asks, coming into the kitchen.

We are all packed, have been for two days, waiting for him to tell us when to go.

"We're ready, Rudi," Klara says. "We have been for days."

"Let's go then," he says.

"Now?" Klara asks.

"Now."

We thank Madame Russier. The children are at school, Monsieur Russier is out with the animals. There is already a thick covering of snow on the ground, so we each put on an extra sweater under our coats. Rudi sees us off here, not wanting to take us to the train station, as there are too many Germans around. It is a quick good-bye—anything else would be too painful. We walk to the station in silence and get on a train heading for Grenoble. Once in Grenoble we see German soldiers everywhere and it's sheer luck we aren't stopped. From Grenoble we go to Annemasse, just on the Swiss border, right across from Geneva. When we get off the train, someone is there to meet us, a young French woman.

"Lisette?" she says to me. That is my fake name.

For a moment I stare at her blankly, then I realize. "Yes. Yes," I say. "And this is Jean, and my friend Marie-Justine."

"Fine, fine," she says, "please follow me. Madame Philip has sent me to you."

"Are you going to take us to the border?" I ask.

"Just follow me," she repeats. We walk through the town until we reach a two-story building. She takes us inside and into a parlor. "This is a Salvation Army house," she says. "I'm sorry to tell you this, but the border has been closed. There are German troops everywhere, and many Jews have already been captured today."

"But we have papers!" Klara objects.

"It doesn't matter," she says. "The Germans have sealed

the border. No one gets across. Not legally, anyway. I don't know what we can do to help you," she says. "I'm afraid you may have to go back to Le Chambon."

"I'm going to try anyway," Peter declares.

"Peter!" I say. "It's stupid. You'll get caught."

"We have to get across the border," he says suddenly. "We'll go at night. We can do it."

"If you're willing to try," Klara says, "so am I."

Has she lost her mind? Little, timid, Klara. It's a good thing I did come along. "Now look here, Klara," I say, "you aren't going anywhere! We'll go back to Le Chambon."

"Rudi wanted us out of there," she says. "You know they'll be looking for us—especially since we disappeared once already. We'll have to stay in hiding this time, no school, just stuck somewhere—waiting. And with all these Germans around we might not even make it back there safely. No," she says fiercely, "I'm going with Peter."

I glare at Peter. "I knew you were trouble the first time I heard you open your mouth," I say to him.

He shrugs. "Just because you don't like what I say doesn't mean it isn't true." He looks me in the eye as he says it.

I shake my head and I have to smile, a little. "You're right," I admit. "It doesn't. All right. I can't let you two go on your own. And actually, it's probably worth the risk. So we'll leave right after dark and see if we can find anywhere to slip across."

The Salvation Army workers feed us some warm soup and give each of us a glass of milk. When it is dark we thank them, and leave. We walk along the country roads but there are patrols and Germans at every border post. Finally we see a farm.

"We're going to take a chance and see if they can help us," I say. "If we stay out here any longer we're sure to get stopped."

Quickly we run to the farmhouse. I knock on the door. A middle-aged woman answers. I say, "I'm sorry to trouble you, Madam, but we need help." I know she can turn us all in if we've been unlucky. She looks at us for a moment, then nods, and opens the door. She takes us to the cellar, and tells us to wait there until morning. She leaves us with a small candle.

It is dark and musty down here, and we have no idea if we are waiting to get picked up by the French police, whom she might have called, or if she's trying to hide us. But we wait. Klara and Peter whisper to each other. I lean on a sack of potatoes and try to rest. It is a long night. I suppose we doze on and off. A rooster crows. Finally, the cellar door opens. A man walks down the steps. He gives each of us a pair of overalls and a pair of wooden shoes. "Put these on," he says. And he leaves.

We do as he asks. When we go upstairs, he says, "You'll have to leave your knapsacks here. They'll give you away." I run and get my briefcase, fold it carefully, and put it in my overall pocket. It's all I have left of my family and I won't leave it behind. We do leave our false papers, though. He gives each of us a huge metal milk can to carry and tells us to make as much racket as possible with them. And he motions us to follow him.

We march across a field, then down a road, which leads straight toward a German border post. My heart is in my throat. Is he going to turn us in? About fifty feet from the post he turns left and follows another path. Out of nowhere, or rather, from behind some pine trees, three Benedictine monks appear. They motion us to follow them. The farmer turns and leaves. The monks take us right up to a high wire fence, which must be on their property. One by one we are boosted over, first Klara, then Peter, then me. As I drop to the ground, the first thing I see is a pair of black jackboots, and the first sound I hear is German: "Halt!" Slowly, I look up. Black boots, grayish green uniform, my heart is pounding, my God, what will happen to us, will we just be shot? Rudi, I'm sorry, I tried to keep Klara safe, please forgive me, if I could only see you one last time. . . . And then I see it. The Swiss cross. It is a German-speaking Swiss soldier.

"What are you doing?" the soldier demands.

"Waiting for a streetcar?" I reply.

He grunts. "This is no time for jokes!" He goes to a field telephone and makes a call. And then he comes back shaking his head. We all look at each other. I take Klara's hand. Peter takes her other hand.

"Come on," the soldier says, "I'm told to take you in to Geneva. They're going to let you stay. I can't keep track," he mutters. "One day it's yes, the next day it's no." He looks at us. "I guess you're just lucky."

But we barely hear him. Because we are hugging and kissing each other and crying. We've escaped the Nazis. They won't get to kill these three Jews, at least.

As we are loaded in the back of the truck I begin to sing from *The Threepenny Opera*:

> *All I'm asking isn't much.*
> *Once, instead of all this mess,*
> *From a man, a little gladness.*
> *Is that asking very much?*
> *Is that asking such a much?*

And the others join in, until we are all singing at the top of our lungs, and we *can*, because for this moment at least, we are free.

But I'm already thinking of Rudi, and the resistance. And of what happened to Mother and Aunt Mina and to Oma. They made a mistake not killing this Jew. Because now this Jew just might come after *them*.

AFTERWORD

When I went to New York to interview those who had been hidden in the village of Le Chambon, I expected short interviews and was thankful that people were willing to talk to me. Never did I expect to be welcomed into the homes of the Lewins and the Liebmanns, fed, and treated with such warmth and generosity. And when Egon Gruenhut shared the diary he had written at the time with me I knew I was dealing with very special people. Afterward, I wondered if their experiences in Le Chambon had somehow rubbed off on them, helping to make them into the extraordinary people that they are. And then Eva Lewin mailed me a letter sent to the Trocmé family in October 1996, when Magda Trocmé died, and I realized that there was a connection. Hanne Liebmann and Elizabeth Koenig wrote the letter, and it was signed by those who had been saved in the village of Le Chambon, and are now living in the United States. With their permission I reprint the letter here:

Dear Magda:

We, your friends, who came to know you during the war years in Le Chambon as Maman Trocmé, and many of our spouses who came to know you after the war, would like to address a few words to you. Words, to tell you how much we came to love and admire you and to tell you what a great influence you had on all of us. Few people are as strong and determined as you have been in doing and showing the untold many what a human being should and can be.

You did so in great humility and modesty and against overwhelming odds.

You have gone from us in a physical sense. Your fighting spirit, courage, and love has always inspired us and even our children. We will always try to live up to

your expectations and be good human beings concerned
with our fellow man not with ourselves.

Adieu, dear friend, from all of us, your extended
family.

With the permission of Nelly Trocmé Hewett, here is a quote from her mother, Magda Trocmé:

"We would not have, rooted in ourselves, the ideal, the hope, the need for justice and love, which we all have, no matter what religion we practice or what degree of civilization we have reached, if somewhere there was not a *source* of hope, of justice, of truth and love—and it is that *source* which I call God."

This was a special place and time in the midst of evil. The bravery and the courage of the people of Le Chambon should never be forgotten. And I will never forget the bravery and courage of the survivors.

My readers often ask if my stories are based on one person, and if they are factual. Historical fiction, is just that, fiction. These characters are made up by me, although occasionally there is a real person interwoven into the story—like Pastor Trocmé, Pastor Theis, and the official Lamirand. The story itself is based on historical research—and in this case quite specifically based on the stories told to me by those to whom I dedicate the book. There are some differences between this story and some other written versions. I can only say that my story is based not only on the reading I did, but largely on interviews with people who were there, and sometimes people remember differently.